THE ICY BARBER

an historical fiction

by

Glennis Leith

Wakelin Partners

Published 2012
Wakelin Partners
PO Box 952, Strathalbyn
South Australia 5255

Cover illustration by
Cultivate Design
PO Box 515, Echunga 5153
South Australia

Printed in Australia by DoctorZed Publishing
www.doctorzed.com

ISBN 978-0-9579341-3-9 (p/bk)
ISBN 978-0-9579341-2-2 (digital)

ACKNOWLEDGEMENTS

This story was inspired by an anecdote relating to an ancestor and his brother who were both Arctic whaling men of the Shetland Islands. My husband and I visited the Shetlands and fell in love with the landscape and the people, so this book begged to be written.

Sincere thanks go to my husband, Colin, my family and friends who urged me onwards over a number of years and who, in reading and commenting on the narrative, contributed in no small way to the result.

My particular thanks go to writer and mentor James Parsons who went through every word of this tale and offered sound support and suggestions that greatly added to the story. Thanks also to Cheryl Jenner, my long-time writing buddy.

It would be remiss of me not to mention the role played by other mentors throughout my writing life: members of writing groups in the Adelaide Hills region, as well as other writers world-wide who inspire me, plus the rewarding support received from professional groups including the South Australian Writer's Centre and the Australian Society of Authors.

THE ICY BARBER

by

Glennis Leith

CHAPTER ONE – *The Leave-taking*

The argument that day in March of 1844 changed everything. Somehow, I knew the voyage would be different and I felt as helpless as a newborn babe. I needed Thorold beside me to give me direction and security, not sailing away to the Arctic after whales. He was my rock, the man I looked to for help and guidance. For the first time in our brief marriage I begged him, though I knew it would not please him.

'Don't go, Thorold, please. Our future is here in the Shetlands amongst our kin,' I said.

Thorold did not pause as he piled his belongings into his sea-chest. 'I'm a whaling man, Inga. You knew that when we married. I've no heart for the land.'

I fluttered about him, for all the world like a bairn begging for a treat. 'It's better than risking your life at sea.'

'Don't fuss, wife. I'm accustomed to it.' He put the last of his things into the chest and fastened it.

'But the ice … it crushes ships as if they were paper.'

'The *Falcon* is a strong ship, Inga, and Captain Walterson a good master.'

I tried a different tack, counting on past grief to persuade him. 'You know I've lost two brothers to the ocean. You were their friend. Only Jacob remains because his life is here, on the land. Please stay with me. I don't want to lose you. I want us to raise a family; I don't want to mourn for what might have been, like so many womenfolk do.'

His face assumed a stern expression, his brown eyes as dark as burnt toffee, his voice firm. 'You won't. Now, stop fretting and wish me fair sailing.' He grasped me about the waist and lifted me to him in a farewell embrace that engulfed me and left me breathless. It was our last farewell.

There was no fair sailing. The ship was lost. Thorold disappeared from my life, taken by the sea as I had feared. My words had sealed his fate, I was sure of it. It was my fault the ship was lost; I was to blame.

~~~~~

The winter of 1844 lashed me until I scarce knew who I was. Alone, where I had once been loved, I waited and hoped for a miracle. I tossed restlessly in my lonely bed and ached for the comfort of Thorold sleeping beside me. I dreamed of his return, though in daylight hours I knew it was in vain. 'Oh, Thorold, my dearest,' I murmured, as if summoning him from the Arctic wastes. I pictured him returning, grizzled but happy, and I imagined rushing into his arms and smelling his skin, feeling the rough stubble on his rugged face as he folded me to him. At night I hugged my dreaming, not wishing to wake, and in the morning I wept bitter tears. 'Why me, Lord? Could I not have had one year, one bairn?' Oh, the pain of it. It crushed my innards and my heart shredded at the few precious memories stored there.

When I ventured out of doors I saw Thorold's figure ahead of me and rushed to greet him, only to be dismayed by another's face. I was haunted by thoughts of the children we might have had, bright little bairns crowding around my skirts and jigging on his knee. My emptiness was a woman's sorrow, fathoms deep. Day after day I forced myself to my routines, having no regard for what I did, and night after night I wept, nursing the pain that never left me. My eyes continually searched the dull horizon for news of Thorold's ship, but months slid by with no word. The *Falcon* failed to return from the Arctic whaling grounds and my hopes dissolved and trickled away like gritty sludge from the last snows. My life was as barren as the slopes around me. I looked at other widows, saw their drooped shoulders and their sad, downcast eyes and knew I had joined them.

~~~~~~

That black winter drifted into a feeble spring and the cycle of life began anew as sea-birds returned to the island shores to nest. There was much to be done and the short northern nights of summer urged me to rise early and labour long. Early each morning I donned petticoats and a plain brown dress that swept the floor. I tied a calico apron around my waist before gathering my hair in a bunch at the nape of my neck and fastening it with a ribbon. The soles on my cowhide rivlins were worn exceedingly thin; they would need replacing before winter though I had nary enough money. Without Thorold's share of the voyage bounty, the savings I had put by were almost gone. I tended the animals, enlarged the walled planticrub where I grew herbs for remedies, and did chores for father on his farm nearby. Hard work turned my thoughts away from Thorold, and I began to take pleasure in the healthy ache of back and limbs at day's end. I was so well occupied that my twenty-fourth birthday passed unremarked, and I barely noticed the arrival of lively autumn winds that swooped and dived across the bald Shetland landscape. I always savoured the milder autumn weather. The morning air was crisp and the low-gliding sun shed a thin light across the slopes behind St Ninian's Bay, making the landscape glow like a sacred painting. It would change when gales stormed across the islands, blasting a mantle of snow that would drive people indoors to warm themselves beside peat fires.

Our croft was heavily scented with herbs. The sweet, aromatic scents overlay the familiar earthy odours of barley, corn, cows and peat. I gained pleasure from grinding herbs and roots and distilling their essences for remedies. I was most at peace among the smells that arose from my distillations. My healing skills were sought by many to relieve their ailments and I was known beyond the local community, such that Doctor Anderson had knowledge of my custom. It made little difference to his practice, as townsfolk needed both medical and surgical skills, but folk in the south more frequently resorted to my concoctions and he was summoned less often as my standing increased.

The mix of heady odours from our croft excited the attention of young Rhona Sinclair. She was of an age to find work, likely gutting herring rather than working the land like her brothers. Rhona hurtled across the moor to our croft on her spindly eleven-year-old legs and watched me as I ground herbs and distilled them. She displayed a lively curiosity about every plant, every method, every use that could be made of the herbs and roots that I gathered. In the long dreary months after Thorold's ship was lost, when I was overcome with the weight of my grief, the child's undemanding presence had been welcome. Rhona's liveliness began to dissolve the chill that immobilised me through that dark time. It was a chill that also lingered in the Sinclair home for they too had lost a son to the sea; it was a chill that Rhona escaped, as I did, by attending to my herbals.

I well understood Rhona's need, for the month I turned seventeen I lost two brothers in a gale at sea. Thorold had been there to comfort me and I was glad of it. He was also there three years later when my older sister, Mary, died within twenty-four hours from the onset of a virulent fever. That bleak and bitter January had been etched deep in my heart.   All our family were stricken by Mary's death. Jacob assumed much of the work on the farm and was more often glum that not.   And ever since that day I kept silent the torment that spread within me like a bloodstain. Like my younger sister, Charlotte, I hadn't contracted the fever and forever felt the burden of guilt. Why did we still live when our beloved and robust older sister did not? While Charlotte was too young to feel such a burden, I felt it should have been me who was taken; it should have been me.   Now, while I was in mourning for my dear lost husband, Rhona appeared and it seemed to me as if an ageless pattern was being repeated, knitting together those that had lost the thread.   I took pleasure in the girl's company, glad to be able to pass to another the skills learned at my mother's knee.

I began to anticipate each day with its simple tasks. The cows stood waiting in the byre so I milked them before feeding the hens and then ate a hurried breakfast of oatmeal porridge. I moved to the stone-walled garden plot beside the croft and focused on the things I would need for the coming winter – snake weed for the bowel and wounds, and a generous supply of thyme to make a nerve tonic. I could hear the hens fussing like gossiping fishwives at the docks.

The croft's thatched stone structure looked like an upturned boat. It was sufficiently distant from Bressay Sound, where the Greenland whalers came into harbour, for me not to smell the boiled-down blubber from their try-pots or hear the screech of scavenging gulls, but the familiar tang of fish hung in the air all around the islands. Crofts were dotted about the bare slopes like scattered knuckle-bones on a field of moss. A light smoke haze hung in the air. Nearby I could see folk working their land, moving stock, cutting peat, and hear the faint but unmistakable sound of children.

Inside the croft, the narrow space between the living quarters and the cattle byre was warm with the fug of animals. I bound the herbs I'd gathered with twine, stood on tiptoe and hung them on a nail above the door to dry. Now, I would need to gather some wild agrimony. Aye, and wallflower and yarrow to put up for winter. I donned a shawl, took a woven straw basket and moved purposefully across the hillside, glad of my skill with herbs. While I could make remedies, I would not become a herring gutter with reddened hands scarred by sharp knives. Nor would I beg for charity at the houses of the gentry. Parochial Board or no, it was the town fathers who dictated who got relief and who did not. I set my jaw. I would not humble myself before those portly gentlemen with their starched collars and gleaming fob watches. My eyes watered in the breeze as, for a moment, I doubted my own word, but these thoughts only served to increase my industry, to gather what was needed before I made my way home. The basket full, I held my apron fast at the corners, resting the harvest in its hollow. The fragrance of freshly picked thyme wafted upwards and, with it, my resolve began rising like nourishing sap.

~~~~~~

As I approached the croft, I saw a figure waiting at the door with his back to the rising wind that swept in from the ocean and scudded across fields of stubble. He was difficult to distinguish but, as I drew nearer, I recognised the lean figure wrapped in a formal black coat with its broad, high collar as the Reverend Tait. I felt my cheeks warm at the sight. His glossy thatch of auburn hair resisted captivity under his hat so he clasped the hat in his hands and stamped fretfully, first one foot, then the other. I sensed him watching me and, aware that he might see a swathe of my scarlet petticoat, I adjusted my skirt to cover the offending splash of colour.

'Good day to you, Reverend. What brings you to my door?'

Reverend Tait bowed lightly in greeting and gestured to the door of the croft. 'I have no wish to trouble you, Missus Jamieson, but I have news to convey – of some importance.'

I led him inside and hung my shawl on a peg. My home was simply furnished with hand-hewn pieces. I glanced around to ensure that everything was in order: the earthenware and everyday utensils were in the timber press beside the door and the deep-sided wooden tub was stored beneath the table. It was my good fortune that I had cleared up after breakfast. Too late, I saw the soiled wash cloth draped over the side of the tub. I moved a chair to hide the offending sight and set the herbs aside on the table: I would deal with them later.

We each took a seat beside the hearth. Reverend Tait rested his hat upon one knee, turning it by the brim with his long, tapered fingers. Furrows creased his face and knots began to coil, unbidden, in my stomach. Whatever news he carried, it was not good news.

'What is it, Reverend? What brings you here?'

He hunched his shoulders and spoke with care as if his words would shed blood.

'Sailors newly arrived in port speak of a lone man taken up from the ice by the *Shearwater*. The ship arrived in Lerwick yesterday.'

I held my breath, my muscles tensed and a sour ball rose in my stomach. I covered my mouth, afraid to utter a sound. The Reverend's wire-rimmed spectacles made his eyes appear huge, blue pools that moved and shifted in the light. The room looked huge as well. I gripped the sides of my chair as everything seemed to tilt, and I feared I might lose my balance.

'Are you alright?' Reverend Tait stretched his hands towards me.

I tried to regain control, measuring my breathing as if trying to recall a lost function. 'I ... I believe so. Please, go on.'

Reverend Tait appeared to watch me closely as he leaned forward on his seat. 'The sailors say the man is from Shetland, hereabouts.'

My mouth was dry and a vein jumped in my temple. 'Might it be Thorold?'

'It appears the man sailed on Thorold's ship, on the *Falcon*.' He hesitated, seeming conscious of the emotions the news aroused in me, then dropped his gaze as he spoke. 'By all accounts, the man is in a sorry condition. He has been long on the ice and ... well, it may be Thorold, but it is difficult to be sure.'

The two of us sat unmoving, like cattle left in rain and sleet, their backs turned against the onslaught that bore down on them. My pulse raced, but whether from excitement or fear, I did not know. My husband ... returned? Memories of Thorold's large warm hands and the rich swell of his laughter rushed into my mind and my heart leapt. But the man must be seriously hurt for his identity to be unclear. I remembered the argument I had with Thorold, only weeks after our marriage, and my control began to fold in upon me. I had felt so small beside his six-foot frame as I pleaded with him to stay and work the family land-holding.

'I would have wished to bring you cheerful news,' Reverend Tait murmured, absently picking at the trim on his hat.

The sound of his voice startled me.

'Inga,' he said, then coloured slightly. 'Missus Jamieson. You ought to prepare yourself and refrain from high expectation lest your hopes come to nothing. Yet, if God pleases, your husband may come home again. If not, the man may perhaps furnish news of Thorold and his ship. It is in God's hands.'

I was cold of a sudden and rubbed my arms and hands to warm them.

'I'll call on your brother and ask him to come.' Reverend Tait rose to take his leave. 'I'll let myself out.'

I was utterly disordered and my mind raced through the possibilities: Thorold's ship was provisioned for much less than a year in the ice. Eighteen months had passed since the *Falcon* sailed in the spring of 1844. How could anyone survive that long in the Arctic without adequate supplies?

That winter had been severe. Storms had raged across the islands and, alone in the croft, I had wept and mourned the loss of my new husband. I had heard whalers talk about the Arctic wind that scoured razor-sharp particles across the ice in a rasping haze that resembled a furnace of steam. They called it the icy barber. It slashed at everything in its path and sailors who ventured into the Arctic likened it to a thousand sharp blades slicing into their flesh. The thought of Thorold battling such conditions gnawed at me. That winter the cold had bitten deeply into my body and heart. For months my grief had almost engulfed me. Now, the news that Thorold may have survived his ordeal revived the pain that I had thought blunted, exhausted beneath the weight of time.

Only a few days earlier, a colossal pod of whales had been driven ashore at Quendale and a crowd had gathered in the hope that the *Falcon* might have been pursuing the

11

monsters of the deep, and thus restore the menfolk to their hearths. But it proved to be the force of nature, not man, that had driven the pod ashore and I, among others, returned to widowhood.

Now I was suspended, as helpless as a grain of sand in an hourglass, not knowing what lay ahead. I rubbed at my tense neck and shoulders, the muscles taut as a towrope. I had been a widow for a year yet the rawness of my loss remained. I glanced across the room at a shelf of bottled preparations, stored against the coming winter, my hope for independence, a salve to my loneliness. Dear God, what if it was Thorold? Perhaps, if it was, he would remain here with me, rather than go whaling again. My heart pounded as I looked to the future. I whimpered with excitement and yet felt the chill of fear as I pressed both hands to my breast.

CHAPTER TWO – *A Lone Survivor*

At last, my brother Jacob arrived. He bulked in the low doorway, his work cap crushed between broad, work-stained hands, an unkempt fringe of dark hair falling like a pony's mane over his brow. His thick eyebrows were drawn down by deep furrows on his forehead.

'You think it's him, don't you?' I asked.

He was blunt, as always. 'Aye, I do.'

'I must go to him. Do you know where he is?'

'At Missus Reid's infirmary. He'll not be a pretty sight, by all accounts. Reverend Tait said the man stank like a cesspit when they brought him in. They had to burn his clothes; they were full of vermin.'

'Vermin? In the Arctic?'

'Aye. Bugs, ye canna see 'til they feed on your flesh.' He scratched his arm as if to rid himself of the blood-sucking creatures.

I shuddered and gripped the sleeves of his heavy jacket. 'Take me to him.'

Outside, the sky was gull-grey. A creeping mist hugged the fields. We climbed into the wooden pony trap that stood outside the door, Jacob lightly flicked the reins on the pony's rump, and we set off towards the town. All over the islands, folk made their own paths across the fields to market squares and fishing haafs. At this time of year the going was soggy from early rains, but not yet a quagmire.

'Hey, there, easy boy.'

Jacob spoke to the pony as to a friend and the animal responded readily to his voice. He guided the pony along familiar contours and rutted tracks, taking care to avoid peat bogs and marshes. The pony strained forward until we crested the hills and the way became easier.

The Shetlands were bare of trees. So, as we travelled, we had an unobscured view of the remote landscape. Small villages and scattered houses were set like decorations on a lightly-tossed counterpane. Horses and cows grazed in the fields. They would be sheltered in byres before winter set in. As we made our way north, I watched a flight of gulls swirl overhead and was swamped with waves of noise that Jacob appeared not to hear. My neck and shoulders stiffened as we moved closer to the town. I wanted to bellow, to bleat, like a young animal. Eight years had passed since Thorold and I had met, eight years that seemed an eternity.

I turned to Jacob. 'Do you remember when Thorold and dear brother Gilbert went whaling together on the *Nelly May*?'

'Aye. And Jerome not long after.'

'I remember when Gilbert introduced me to Thorold.' I savoured the memory, and the warmth of it evoked a smile. Thorold's brown eyes had pinned me like a prized butterfly for his collection. And I was free, sixteen years of age and not spoken for.

Jacob grinned. 'You were impudent, as I recall. Powerful sure of yourself.'

I laughed as I remembered teasing Thorold: 'Are you sure you're a whaler? You're not a tax collector, an inspector of some kind?' I remembered being surprised by his fruity laughter.

'They were good days,' I said now.

Thorold and I were wed in the winter following my twenty-second birthday, when Thorold was twenty-six. I recalled our solemn marriage vows and the clear moonlit night that followed, a cover of freshly fallen snow blanketing the landscape. So brief the happiness, so fleeting the loving in our warm box bed. It was only four short months before he went whaling again. Now, as Jacob and I travelled towards Lerwick, I could smell the tang of the ocean and shivered. I glanced uncertainly at my brother, conscious of the hesitancy in my voice.

'If I'm to care for Thorold, restore him to health and find provisions for us both, I'll not be able to help father as I do now.'

Jacob kept his focus on the way ahead. 'No matter. Norah will help.'

'She has her hands full with the bairns.'

He paused before responding. 'Norah will do it,' he said and flicked the reins briskly on the horse's rump.

I shifted myself on the seat. 'I owe you much for your patience.'

'You're kin.' He glanced sideways and fold lines forked at the corners of his grey eyes. 'We were glad when you turned to making home remedies again.'

I kept my gaze on my hands. 'Just as I did after Mary was taken by the fever.'

'Aye.' His open, ruddy face appeared careworn.

'It's a good restorative, caring for others.'

Eighteen months earlier, Thorold and I had conjured up dreams of a full life. Now I yearned for that life again, without the dread of poverty. My days were full tending animals, growing herbs, preparing remedies, together with domestic chores. How could I nurse a sick man as well, with so little money? I would not throw myself on charity or gut fish for a living. For the remainder of the journey, I contemplated how I would manage, if Thorold had truly returned from the edge of death. I bunched my fists. I would find a way, that I would, I vowed. Thorold's strength held me fast before; now it was my turn to hold fast.

~~~~~

Hours later, Jacob and I arrived on the outskirts of Lerwick, breathless from our travel against the wind. The pony had begun to grow his rough winter coat and a feathery sheen of sweat lay over the coarse pelt. Jacob guided the trap onto a narrow street that curved downhill to the harbour. Two-storey stone and granite buildings flanked either side of the street and circled the clearing around Market Cross that opened to the harbour. Anchored in Bressay Sound were a number of square-rigged sailing ships, while closer in to the harbour smaller herring boats were moored. Not far along the waterfront was a grey granite structure that served as Missus Reid's infirmary. Set in its substantial walls were small many-paned windows that shed a timid light into the building's cold rooms.

Missus Reid greeted us at the panelled timber door, her sleeves pushed above her elbows, a crisp white apron clinging to her ample bosom and formidable hips.

'You've arrived barely in time,' she said.

We halted, unsure what events might have overtaken us.

'The man is severely frostbitten. One foot must come off if we are to save the leg, and the toes of the other as well.' I felt the colour flee from my face. I slumped against Jacob and hung onto his arm for support. Missus Reid looked directly at Jacob. 'Doctor Anderson is here. He'll be glad of your help.'

'What do you want me to do?' Jacob was a farmer, comfortable with livestock and their ailments, but unfamiliar with the realm of human medicine.

'We've only John, the yardman, to hold him down.' She looked at me. 'There'll be blood. It must be swabbed clear while Doctor operates.'

'Oh, God. I ... I don't know if I can.' I trembled, my eyes restless, searching for an escape.

Missus Reid's steel-grey hair presided over a face that resembled the contours of one of the rocky outcrops that dropped sheer to the ocean around the islands. She narrowed her eyes, as if assessing us, as we stood silent in front of her. 'You'll do. Follow me.'

She flurried ahead and ushered us into a cold room. A bare table stood in the centre. Alongside, on a smaller table, was equipment that seemed to me more fitting to a blacksmith than an infirmary. I preferred my world of herbal physic but reluctantly acknowledged that extreme situations demanded extreme measures. I was transfixed by the array of cutting, sawing and stitching instruments, most of which were unfamiliar to me. I began to breathe heavily at the thought of what they could do. Against one wall was a stone-topped side table with a basin and ewer of water. Nearby, leaning against the wall, was a pail and mop.

'Here, put these on.' Missus Reid supplied us with large aprons. 'Take off your footwear, and roll up your sleeves.'

Jacob stuffed his boots into his jacket pockets. My feet were bare of shoes. My hands were clammy and my fingers fumbled trying to tie the apron. 'Where is he?'

Jacob tied the strings behind me. 'We'll see him soon enough.'

At that moment, a burly older man entered the room. He had the gnarled appearance of one who spent a lifetime out of doors. A limp figure was slung over his shoulder. 'Lend an 'and 'ere,' the yardman said to Jacob, and the two of them carefully lay the barely conscious man on the table. The smell of whisky rolled powerfully through the room.

I stepped forward, holding my breath in fear, and halted abruptly at the sight that confronted me. 'Oh, dear God.' My stomach heaved at the smell of decay from the figure on the table. This was definitely my husband, Thorold, but there was scarcely any resemblance to the man I had married.

He had no eyebrows. Matter oozed from the corners of eyes that appeared milky and sightless. His nose and lips were ravaged as if eaten away by ferocious beasts, and what remained of his ears was black. Thorold's skin, what I could see of it, was leathery and scarred, reminding me of hide left untended in the field. I glanced at his feet and my throat constricted. I was sickened by the putrid flesh, hideous colours signalling the immutable advance of gangrene.

'Oh, Lord, I can't.' My whole body shook and began to fold and Jacob took hold of my arm.

'Steady there, lass. He needs you.'

'Are we all ready, then?' Doctor Anderson entered the room, a stockily built man with greying hair, a barrel chest and an oversize nose. Missus Reid wrapped a protective apron around his ample frame. 'My, my. It's a piteous creature we have here. I'm given to understand he may be your husband, Missus Jamieson?'

19

I gulped. 'It is indeed my husband, though he's barely recognisable.'

Doctor Anderson looked at the figure awaiting his attention. 'Quite. As you can see, one foot is gangrenous and the toes of the other. His overall condition is poor as a consequence of his time on the ice. I regret the necessity for this. It could be the end of him, but without it he'll certainly not live.'

Tears flooded my eyes. They blurred my vision and I struggled to blink them away. I'd need to keep my wits about me in this charnel house.

Doctor Anderson glanced at Jacob. 'Give John some assistance there, lad.'

John stood on one side of the table, Jacob on the other, holding down Thorold's hips and legs. I stood beside Jacob and Missus Reid stood opposite, each of us restraining Thorold's arms and upper torso. Doctor Anderson took up a hideously-toothed saw, checked the condition of its blade, and set himself beside Jacob at the lower end of the table, spreading his feet slightly for balance.

Nobody spoke. I was sure the temperature had dropped. My feet were icy and there was insufficient air in the room. Alcoholic fumes rose from Thorold's comatose form and began to fog my brain. I heard a faint whirring sound, like a flock of birds soaring overhead, and everything lost colour. Doctor Anderson set the saw against Thorold's left leg, at mid-calf above his blackened foot, and began to draw the saw through flesh and bone.

Blood poured onto the floor and doused our feet, its metallic smell mixing with the sickening odour of fetid flesh, bone-dust and sweat. Through a shroud of alcohol, Thorold's brain must have registered the horrendous assault on his body, stretching him, like burning taffy, straight to the maw of hell. He screamed and thrashed about, his blood-curdling shrieks carrying clear into town and across Bressay Sound before, mercifully, unconsciousness claimed him. At Thorold's first cry, I froze, my blood stopped in its veins. The room whirled about me and I collapsed on the bloodied floor.

When I regained consciousness, the grisly task was done and Jacob crouched beside me, cradling me against his chest. Our clothing was sprayed with blood. I could see Thorold's foot where it had been dumped in a bucket with his toes, and quickly averted my eyes.

'Thorold ... is he ...?'

'He's still with us.'

Jacob wiped blood from my feet with his untied apron, and helped me to stand.

'Jacob,' I sobbed, 'What are we to do?'

'Nought but pray. It's in the Lord's hands.'

Doctor Anderson and Missus Reid were busy suturing Thorold's wounds and dressing them before he could be returned to bed. I staggered to the corridor, supported by my brother.

Later, when I had recovered some of my composure, Missus Reid appeared at the door, erect and formal, with Doctor Anderson a step behind her. He was wiping his hands on one of Missus Reid's hand-hemmed cloths and nodded at me. I was slowly regaining warmth, my face and hands returning to their normal colour, although I continued to shiver.

'Right then,' he said, his manner hurried, 'I've done all I can. It depends entirely on his constitution now.'

I considered I ought to feel gratitude for this man's services, but I was repulsed by his brisk manner, as if he separated limbs from his patients as a matter of course. I hesitated to ask, but had to know. 'What chance of recovery does my husband have?'

He continued to wipe his plump, pink hands. 'I can't guarantee he'll recover. His general condition is poor. We'll have to wait and see.' He passed the soiled cloth to Missus Reid. 'Good day,' he said and flashed a thin smile at the three of us as he left.

~~~~~

Jacob and I sat beside Thorold's bed and waited anxiously for him to regain consciousness. I detected the odour of his weeping wounds and tried to ignore the bloodstains that seeped through the sheets. Once or twice I reached towards Thorold's bandaged hands but stopped short of touching them, concerned not to disturb or startle him and, at the same time, somewhat repulsed by the thought of what lay beneath.

Thorold's breathing was laboured, ragged and soughing like waves breaking against the cliffs; his skin was overlain with a pallid sheen. Occasionally he moved his head and made unintelligible sounds full of pain. My eyes brimmed with tears as I looked at his sea-ravaged condition. He seemed to me as foreign as any stranger, resembling nothing of the man who had left our home eighteen months earlier to go whaling. Tears tracked down my cheeks and left my face wet.

Thorold stirred and his eyelids fluttered. I leaned forward and murmured, 'Thorold, it's me ... Inga.' He turned his head slightly towards me, but appeared not to know who I was. 'I doubt he knows me, Jacob. Does he know where he is? Does he remember anything, do you think?'

Jacob screwed up his face, as if flinching from his imaginings. 'Of the blade?'

I shook my head. 'No, I'd not wish that on him. But, does he remember the *Falcon* ... what happened to it, what happened to him and the rest of the crew?' Jacob's hands rested on my shoulders.

'He was feeble when they found him. It'd be a miracle if his memory was whole.'

Abruptly, Thorold cried out. The sound shredded our composure.

'Dear God, this is a nightmare.' I twisted my damp handkerchief until it was knotted tightly in my hands.

Jacob stroked my shoulder. 'There's nought we can do but what's been done.'

We watched Thorold until eventually the pain overtook him and he lapsed again into unconsciousness.

Missus Reid awaited us in the hall, her expression restrained. 'My condolences, Missus Jamieson.' I was galvanised by the woman's words.

'He's with us yet, Missus Reid.'

Missus Reid lifted one corner of her mouth. 'Man proposes, God disposes,' she said and lightly folded her arms across her chest. Jacob and I left the infirmary and stepped into the street, grateful to breathe chilled air that wafted familiar sea-salt and fish odours across the town.

CHAPTER THREE – *Inside the Maelstrom*

Jacob returned to his farm but I stayed in the town to be close to Thorold and keep watch over his progress. In a few days, Thorold's fever began to settle and he accepted light nourishment. Though his suffering appeared to lessen, he complained of a constant, gnawing ache that occasionally sent a shaft of pain up his legs. I tended him lovingly, as any wife would, bathing him, feeding him and reading to him when he appeared lucid and rested. As the days passed, he continued to improve, his scars gradually lost their angry colour and his skin took on a healthier cast. Missus Reid changed Thorold's dressings until his wounds healed and became clean and pink. Doctor Anderson was gratified that his patient was likely to make a satisfactory recovery and would be able to move about with the aid of sticks. I was uplifted to be told that I could take Thorold home.

'He will need a great deal of care,' Doctor Anderson said. Then, his voice gruff, he added, 'Here is my account. Pay me when you can, but ...' He held one finger aloft. '... don't delay too long.'

'Thank you, Doctor,' I muttered and slipped the account into my pocket.

~~~~~

I made haste to the croft above St Ninian's Bay in order to ready it for Thorold's return. Jacob crafted a pair of strong crutches for his brother-in-law, carefully whittling the struts to a clean finish and encasing the tips and armrests in strong leather to reduce wear. My anxiety was diverted by all the preparations. Nevertheless, I felt relieved when Jacob and I eventually set off in the horse and cart to fetch Thorold from the infirmary, leaving the others of our family at the croft. Father leaned on Jacob's wife, Norah, for support as they bade us goodbye, while Charlotte gathered the bairns to her side and watched from the doorway.

Thorold had lost his muscular build. He was pale and weak, not yet accustomed to walking with sticks, and required Jacob's assistance to struggle clumsily to the cart. He was a piteous sight as he lay exhausted on the thick layer of heath and pillows I had piled into the cart. He braced himself as the trap bumped over cobbles on its way south out of the town and appeared more at ease when our path began to incline gently downwards. I hoped that, from his vantage point in the rear of the cart, he might see the rolling green countryside as we left it behind and be glad at the sight of home.

Soon we turned south-west and headed across the Clift Hills, reaching the crest as the sun's shadows began to lengthen. Jacob's daughters, Morna and Georgina, raced to meet us and fell into step beside the horse and cart, like a pair of faithful puppies.

'Why does he have his eyes shut?' four-year-old Morna asked.

'He's tired and doesn't want to talk,' I told her.

'Why is he making that noise?'

'He's hurting. Can you ease the pony a bit, Jacob? The padding doesn't seem enough.'

Jacob hauled on the reins. 'It's as well we're not slipping in ice and snow with a storm howling at our backs.'

The bairns watched Thorold with tender concern as we moved slowly across the mellow hills and down the slopes towards St. Ninian's Bay.

~~~~~

As Jacob and I approached my home, with Thorold stretched out in the trap behind us, I could see Norah waiting for us, her dark blue dress setting off her straight, fair hair that was caught in a twist beneath her cap. She knitted feverishly, as if to cast off cares. Charlotte paced beside her, seeming impatient for us to arrive. Father sat on a stool near the wall and smoked a pipe. We were close enough to wave and then the bairns left our side and ran ahead to join their mother.

'We'll no let him be cassen awa,' father said, his bushy beard and pipe shaking at the pronouncement. 'The sea'll no' get this'n.'

He stepped forward to help Jacob unload the patient and Thorold allowed the two of them to carry him inside while Norah, Charlotte and I followed with the bairns.

The sleeping space at the end of the croft behind the chimney held our big box bed, a smaller bed, a few storage chests, a wooden chair and a stool. Gently they put Thorold on the smaller bed, pulled the quilt up to cover him, then left the room while I tended to him. I had woven a cage of basket canes to keep the pressure of the bedclothes from Thorold's legs. He was pale and damp with perspiration from the strain of the journey, and I wiped his brow with a soft cloth.

'I'll fetch a herbal posset. It'll warm your blood and ease your discomfort.'

Thorold was unresponsive. I knew the journey had not been easy.

In the other room, father and Jacob sat by the hearth smoking their pipes and watched Morna and two-year-old Georgina play cat's cradle with a ball of twine, while Norah and Charlotte fussed over preparations for a meal. I joined them, fetched a bottle of straw-coloured liquid from a shelf and measured two spoonfuls into a beaker. I added hot water from the kettle that hung over the hob.

'If I can settle him to sleep I'll be less anxious.' I took the posset to Thorold who drank it, heaved a long sigh and closed his eyes. I left him sleeping and rejoined the others.

In the parlour conversation was subdued. 'The last time we shared a meal with Thorold at home was a happier time,' Norah remarked. 'God grant it will be so again.'

'It will, if I hae anything to do wi' it,' father declared.

~~~~~

That night, in the midst of sleep, I was woken, my rest ripped apart by Thorold crying out and lurching upright. He flailed about in the darkness while my heart bleated in my chest, like a frightened lamb lost in the snow.

'What was that?!' he cried. 'The wind outside shears through the shrouds and howls across the ice. The bleaching cold freezes the marrow in my bones.'

'It's nothing, Thorold. You've been having a nightmare.'

'Is that a woman's voice?' he asked.

'It's me. Inga,' I replied.

'A woman has no place aboard a whaling vessel, though a wife has been known to accompany the captain aboard ship. Women only add to our burden.'

He obviously thought himself aboard the *Falcon* again. Was there nothing I could do?

'Listen! There it is again. It screeches, like an infernal demon caught by the tail. Surely you can hear it now?'

'What is it, Thorold? What do you hear?'

'Have you stopped up your ears? Do you not understand? That sound ... it's the mast – the main mast is down! The ship's breaking up!'

'But you're not aboard ship, Thorold. You're home.'

'Home. Ah, would that it was so. It's delusion to think it in this dark place.'

His fearfulness unsettled me and all I wanted to do was wrap my arms about him and comfort him. But then he began to shout.

'All hands on deck! We must save the ship!' He pitched out of bed and yelled, 'My feet! I can't feel my feet – they're frozen!'

I stepped from the bed and made to fetch a warming posset for him. 'Come, Thorold. I'll get you a draft of something to help you sleep.'

But he was down on the floor, scrabbling at the timbers, blocking my way. 'There'll be no sleep this night. The dread sickness has laid waste our numbers. There are few hale enough to work. Those who cannot will die. Help me! For God's sake, help shore up the timbers against the ice or we are doomed.'

I could only suppress my heartache and coax him back to bed and to sleep, humouring his delusion. It took some time for Thorold to settle again, and I began to be afraid for his mind, as for his body.

~~~~~~

I felt as if plunged into a maelstrom. Thorold's wounds were healing remarkably well, but fevered night visions jangled him awake and gave neither of us rest. I dosed him with yarrow, comfrey salves and a twice-daily draught

of feverfew but it permitted no more than an hour or two
of sleep.   His nightmares were stormy and often
frightening, but during the day I felt equally oppressed by
his moods that swung unpredictably between deep, silent
gloom and sudden anger, neither of which reflected the
man I once knew. I became increasingly troubled by his
condition. The doctor had said a full recovery was not
guaranteed but made no mention of nightmares.   The
Falcon's last voyage was a constant torment to Thorold,
night after night, until I, too, became taken up with
thoughts of the ship.   What happened on that voyage?
What happened to the ship and the men aboard her?
Thorold's nightmares and mood changes threw a pall over
the croft that matched the darkening skies and troubled me
day and night.

Daylight hours shrank as yet another winter
approached, and the differences between day and night
became less discernible. The horizon was often smudged
against the sky and the pale sun held no warmth.   It
seemed to match the mood in our home. I concentrated on
household routines, balanced my time between tending to
Thorold and earning enough to meet our immediate needs,
with no hope of any savings. I milked the cows, watered
and fed the animals, collected eggs, stacked peat in the
mouldie hoose, ground corn and gathered and dried herbs.
In the evenings, after preparing remedies, I sat spinning
and knitting garments for sale, while fish hung from the
mantel to smoke over the peat fire.

Thorold preferred to keep his own company and retired as soon as he might. His general health steadily improved and he moved about more freely on the crutches Jacob made. But as swiftly as his physical health improved, his spirits sank lower. I was determined to meet his needs without complaint, anticipating that over time, as memories faded, he would regain his positive outlook. Each morning before starting my chores I prepared sufficient food for the day and ensured that whatever else he may need was close at hand. I returned at mid-afternoon to share a simple meal of potatoes and fish with him, but often he was uncommunicative and left the house to sit alone outside, despite the cold, until I resumed my tasks. By the end of the day I was exhausted and ill-prepared to contend with Thorold's moods.

'You don't care about me,' Thorold grumbled as he sat by the hearth, while I sat spinning fleece.

'I do care.'

'I need you here, not traipsing about the countryside.'

I did not pause as a rolag of fleece passed through my fingers, and my feet kept a steady rhythm as thread formed on the wheel. 'Thorold, I can't stay with you all day and, when I am home, you seem to prefer your own company.'

Thorold glared at me. 'Your place is here.'

I eased the pedal long enough to slow the fleece and looked straight at him. 'There are things to be done, and only me to do them.'

Thorold leaned forward and grasped me by the wrist, waving one of his crutches at the row of herbal preparations on the shelf. 'You've time enough for your herbs.'

His tone was both petulant and hostile and I tried to remain calm, although my stomach objected.

'My herbs help to supply our needs, for the moment at least.'

'Are you saying I'm no good as a provider?' His thin face took on the scowl of a wild creature. 'Answer me. Are you?'

I dare not remark on the bounty that was lost with the *Falcon.* 'As things stand you can do nought. You need to regain your strength and then ...'

'Ah, so that's it. I'm nothing to you but a workhorse.'

'You've endured a terrible ordeal, Thorold. Be patient. Better days will come.'

Thorold's mood continued black and I was thankful that he hadn't erupted into violence as so often happened since his homecoming. But my relief was untimely for this night proved no different.

'Damn the lot of ye!' he shouted and took up his crutches, swinging them wildly like some northern invader.

I had taken to storing the earthenware behind the washtub, out of the reach, but I knew what was coming next and fled to the byre. He may be somewhat lame, but when his anger boiled up, all I could do was block my ears against his yells and the sound of breakage.

'Avast there!' I heard him yell. 'I'll have your hide!' And there followed the sound of something breaking.

After an hour or so the croft quietened down and I returned to the living quarters and cleaned up the mess. Thorold had retired, leaving me free to take up a book of miscellany to read. It was difficult to concentrate on the words but I needed to do something to quieten myself. I felt my shoulders and spirits sag but continued reading until I was ready to climb into the box bed. Yet even so, Thorold lay awake and watched me prepare for sleep. 'You're a puny woman – what can you do to change fate?'

I felt my anger rise, despite my best efforts, as Thorold clutched the counterpane to his chest. My tone was less than friendly. 'I'm doing all I can, all I know, to bring us through this.'

He snorted. 'Heaven spare us.'

'You'd best pray that it will,' I snapped as I blew out the lamp.

Throughout the night Thorold's unrest again disrupted our sleep and, by morning, though I was not refreshed, I was glad to rise and get the day under way. I milked the cows and fed the hens, then busied myself in the but end of the croft, wanting to leave before sun-up. I stood the kollie lamp on the mantel as Thorold woke. Moments later he joined me in the parlour and resumed his attack.

'So, you're off doing Lord knows what again.' His gruffness threatened to erupt into anger.

My own emotions flared in response. 'Indeed,' I snapped.

'Is that a proper way to speak to your husband?'

A knock on the door startled us.

I took a lamp to the door where Lillian Isbister and her young daughter, Ellen, stood on the threshold with a lantern, clutching their thin clothes about them in the pre-dawn mist.

'Missus Jamieson. We didn't want to bother you in your misfortune but ... how is Mister Jamieson faring?'

'Um, Missus Isbister. Thank you for asking. Would you care to come in? It's sharpish out at this hour.'

Lillian shifted from one foot to the other, pulled her shawl close around her and rubbed her mittened hands together. Her small daughter huddled against her mother's legs. 'Thanks, but I'll no' stay. I've chores to do and no' much time to spare. I only wanted to ask about Mister Jamieson.'

'The truth is, he's poorly. His wounds have healed but he doesn't move about easily and he's getting very little sleep. More rest would be a boon for both of us.'

'Aye. I can see you're weary. But ... I wonder, has he said anything about the ship, about the crew? Him that belonged to me, the bairns' father, was on the *Falcon* and we'd like ... we need ...' Her eyes moistened.

I felt the torment of Lillian's struggle to avoid mention of her lost husband's name for fear of inviting further disaster and sorrow, a belief difficult to defy. She had three children under the age of eight: Iain, Nicholas and young Ellen. The boys worked in the fields cutting peat while Lillian worked as a washerwoman and forced her chapped and reddened hands to knit fine stockings for sale.

I saw in her my own predicament, had Thorold and I produced a bairn.

'I'm sorry, Lillian. There's mickle Thorold says, even in his sleep, that could tell us of their fate.' I lowered my voice. 'And what little remains of his memory is disordered.'

Lillian brushed her hands across her eyes, while the small girl clutched at her mother's skirts. 'If he says anything … something that … maybe he ...'

'If he tells anything of the ship and its men, I will be sure to pass it on.' I clasped the woman's cold hands between my own. 'For now, we might count it a blessing that they are released from whatever misery brought my husband to this.' I paused. 'I'm not sure which is to be preferred.'

Lillian recoiled, her eyes wide. 'You'd wish your husband dead?'

'No, no, I didna mean that. It's only that he suffers greatly, in body and in spirit. I'd wish him out of his torment.'

'Aaaagh! '

Both of us were startled by the cry from within. Ellen appeared frightened.

'Oh, please excuse me, Missus Isbister. Thorold needs me. I must tend to him.'

Lillian pacified her daughter. 'Of course, Missus Jamieson. Of course.' The woman and child glanced towards the room where Thorold's cries deepened and despair was plain on her face. 'If we knew something of their fate, it'd surely ease my heart.'

The two of us embraced briefly, while the girl's dark eyes watched. Lillian and Ellen walked away into the early dawn, the woman holding her daughter's tiny hand. I remained at the croft door, reluctant to go inside until the two of them were out of sight, and wondered by what demon's design we lived like this. Women scrimped to feed their fatherless families and yearned for the men they had lost. And here I was with this man ... my husband ... yet I barely knew him. What good was survival, if it was like this?

I trudged indoors and sat directly opposite Thorold, aware that he had heard Lillian Isbister's words and had deliberately disrupted our conversation. I tried to draw from his aggrieved expression something of the fate of the men aboard the *Falcon*.

'What am I to tell them, Thorold? What am I to say to the families who come to our door for news of their loved ones?' Thorold turned his face away from me and made a strangled sound. I pressed him for a response. 'Tell me what happened, Thorold. Tell me ... please.' I moved to lay a hand on his arm but he shrugged it away.

'Don't,' he snapped.

I reined in my frustration, tried to come to terms with his reluctance to talk. 'It must pain you, the remembrance. It must be dreadful.'

Thorold yelled at me, sweeping one arm towards the door. 'You know nothing! Leave me. Go!' He turned his back on me and hunched up as much as his tall frame allowed, withdrawing to a silent place I could not reach. I had been banished and could do nothing to breach the divide between us. Eventually, I gave up trying to reach him and went about my daily tasks, knowing there was little prospect of enlightenment. That night I spent the evening hours alone by the fire while Thorold went early to bed.

～～～～～

Not long after we were abed, Thorold again began talking in his sleep. 'There'll be whales to the north of Davis Strait, my lad, mark my words.'

I gently touched his shoulder and said, 'You're at home, Thorold.'

'What's that you say, young 'un? I'm at home? Aye, I've long been at home on the ocean.'

I sighed and sat watchful through his ramblings.

'We're bearing north of Disco Island now. I know it's late in the season and the sea ice presses down on us, but Captain Walterson is a bold driving man and he'll see us safe.'

I murmured, 'You are safe, Thorold,' in the hope of keeping him calm.

'If it pleases God, a week or two more will see us with a goodly haul and by August we'll make a heading for home. If the ice doesn't get us first.'

'You have nothing to fear from the ice, Thorold,' I ventured.

'Ho, there lad. There's plenty to fear from sea ice; that much I know, you green young pup but then, you're new at whaling. Aye, the ice moves like a living thing, its glassy peaks and hidden depths slink along, ever so casually, like a necklet of marshmallow in a cobalt blue pond.'

Thorold's words had a soothing effect on me. There were moments when I felt the appeal of the milky blue ice he talked about.

'In these latitudes, with a glimmer of light for nigh on twenty hours a day, you can see icebergs wander beside us, like ghostly companions. And it's as well we can see them, for the noise of the ice would otherwise alarm us!'

'The ice makes a noise?' I asked, becoming intrigued by his words.

'Aye. If it's not grinding and mashing its mountainous molars together, it's cracking and thundering as massive sheets of ice split asunder, as if from a lightning strike. It's enough to make a body quake and quiver. It's all well and good for you to be agog, you green stripling – but the ice is fearsome. I know its ways.'

Thorold sat nodding his head, seeming comfortable in his whaler's role, and I remained content to listen.

'There's nary enough wind to fill the sails now and the ice is settling against the hull. Keep looking for leads of clear water, lad, to float the ship free. If the ice continues bearing down on us, we're in danger of being held fast. We'd be obliged to pull the *Falcon* to keep her moving, keep her free. I'll warrant you will not enjoy the harness.' He chuckled and the sound gladdened my heart. But Thorold's amusement quickly turned to something darker.

'Ho, then … it's as I feared. We're caught fast. Here, put this on, lad. We'll make a whaler of you yet. There's more to whaling than harpooning and flensing.'

His hands groped about my shoulders as he talked.

'I'd hoped never to wear the harness again, tracking on foot across the ice. But needs must as the Devil drives. And I'm to set the example for the crew. So haul, men! Haul! Put your back into it.'

'What are you doing, Thorold?' I asked, unable to believe what wearing a harness suggested.

'We haul the ship over the ice, drawing her forward inch by agonising inch. The rough edges of the hard straps chafe as we haul her. In God's sight we must look like ants, dragging a huge flying beetle to the nest. And she leaves a snail's track as we lug her forward. It's a mystery before God and man how we do it. But once shifted, even an inch, the ship will work with us.'

I was astonished at the men's strength of will.

'Keep your eyes on your feet, lad. Get a firm grip and lean into it or you'll take your measure on the ice.'

'But the pain, Thorold. Surely it is a painful task.'

'Aye. My feet are numb, past feeling. Pain strikes me at all points and makes my eyes water. My breath condenses as it leaves my nostrils and mouth, and crystallises on my nose and face – my skin cracks under its icy touch. God's truth! It feels like I'm the only one to put my shoulder to the task, though we're twenty men each, on port and starboard sides. Pull, men. Pull! Ease her along.'

'And did the ship move?'

'Aye, it does. We tug, and haul with all our might, and the ship moves forward slowly, reluctantly. Cattle have it easier than whaling men. Sweat dribbles under my clothing and sears as it freezes against my skin. Would that we could find a free lead of water to Baffin Bay. If we are beset, the ice could crush our ship like a bairn's toy underfoot. Heave! Heave, ho! You'll have your rest when the ship is safe – or die trying.'

I was in awe of my husband and the things he had seen and done. At last, exhausted from living again, as if it was real, the experience of hauling the whaling ship over the ice, Thorold and I, too, returned to sleep.

CHAPTER FOUR – *Shoring up Faith*

For a while after news went abroad that Thorold had been found, returned as if from the dead, Rhona's mother, Missus Sinclair, stopped Rhona coming to the croft in deference to our altered circumstances. No doubt Missus Sinclair meant well. But where my life had been busy and fulfilling, communing with friends and neighbours, easing their burdens, delighting in Rhona's newfound skills, and balancing workaday chores with making herbal remedies, it was now isolated and deeply troubled. Young sister Charlotte was occupied with chores at home and when they were done she helped Laurence Gifford, a young widower whose wife had not survived birthing. He had two small bairns and welcomed the assistance that Charlotte was so willing to give. I longed for Charlotte's company, as much as for Rhona's, but she was making her own way in life and I must do likewise. My muscles ached from the work required to make ends meet, supporting two from the labour of one, and my heart ached with loneliness and the loss of a hearty wedded life. What was I to do? I was all the time weary. There was no joy in life. Sometimes I feared my mind was as tangled as Thorold's.

I recalled Rhona and her bounce and chatter and felt myself close to tears. I could not do this alone. I needed Rhona's help and ... I missed the girl. I resolved to ask for her return.

Marian Sinclair came to the door at my knock, house cloth in hand, her pale blue eyes startling in her ruddy complexion. 'Missus Jamieson, ye're a sight to behold. How is Mister Jamieson?'

'He is making a slow recovery, Missus Sinclair.'

'I've no doubt he'll improve wi' your help. We wish ye well in your troubles. What can I do for ye?'

'Since you ask, I've come about Rhona. She may be ... that is, I wonder ... does she continue with her interest in herbals? Has she other things to occupy her, perhaps?'

'None at all, I shouldna think. I've kept her at home since Mister Jamieson returned. Ye'd no need of a body bustling about at such a time. But since he appears to be settling and if ye hae need of her, I'll hae a word wi' her. I shouldna wonder she'll be off in a flash – she's one for dabbling in this 'n that. Are ye sure she'll be no trouble?'

'No trouble at all. I'd be glad of the company and any help she can offer. The season's advancing and I need to put down a good supply of preparations.'

'Aye, thank ye again for Harald's tonic. He's doin' well since.'

'That's a blessing. Let me know if you need more.'

'I'll be sure to, mark my words.'

I felt relief wash over me. 'I'm much obliged, Missus Sinclair. I'm looking forward to seeing Rhona again.'

On my return to the croft, I found Thorold thrashing about on the floor in a tangle of bedding.

'Thorold! What are you doing? What's amiss?'

'The shroud – I'm caught in the shroud!'

Thorold obviously thought himself on the ship again, though it was day. It couldn't be a nightmare this time and he seemed otherwise lucid. I squatted and unwound the sheets that were twined around him.

'Here, put your arm over my shoulder and I'll help you.' I clasped my arm around his waist and lifted as he hauled himself back onto the bed. He trembled and gasped for breath, eyes and nose moist and hands chilled from exposure.

'The shrouds are icy. Robbie Isbister ... he slipped.'

He appeared to accept my presence despite his continuing delusion. I paused and considered how much I should humour him, how far I should support his flawed perception. 'You were up among the sails?'

'Almost at the top of the main mast. Robbie fell.' He was clearly agitated. 'He almost took me with him. I heard ...' He shuddered, turned his head away from me, and I saw the length of his body tremble violently.

I imagined the thud, the bone-crushing thwack of a solid man falling onto a ship's icy deck and I, too, shuddered.

Thorold's brows crimped together. 'Robbie. Is he ..?'

'I don't know, Thorold.'

'I need to know – is he with us or no.'

I felt a headache begin to grip my temple and throb. 'Rest now. I'll go and see what I can find out and return soon.'

I needed to discuss this with someone but Charlotte was never around. All her spare time was taken up with Laurence and the bairns. Her devotion was admirable but I desperately needed to sort out the chaos that was whirling around me. If I could talk through my troubles, perhaps with Reverend Tait ... I knew he would keep my confidences. The thought was father to the deed – I donned a cap and shawl and hurriedly set out for the Manse, across the lean and grey fields, conscious of a deepening sense of foreboding and warring thoughts churning in my mind. How much of what Thorold said was truth? Robbie Isbister – did he truly fall from the mast? Lillian Isbister would welcome word of his fate, but what could I say to her? Should I even raise the possibility? It would seem a mischief to rely on Thorold's ramblings. My thoughts gave me no comfort. I increased my pace across the fields, pushing into the wind.

~~~~~

The manse stood firm against the horizon, a modest yet sturdy stone building of two rooms with a detached corn mill, barn and stable. A small neatly-edged garden and a henhouse relieved the dour facade. Missus Catherine Tait responded to my knock. Her cheeks glowed with vitality and, despite her thickening waist, she appeared dainty and immaculate. In one hand she held a piece of knitting, appearing reluctant to put it down even for an instant.

'Inga, how lovely to see you. Do come in,' Catherine said and beckoned me inside. 'Hallam is composing the Sunday sermon and ... um ... I'm preparing for ...' She blushed.

My mood was lifted for a moment by Catherine's cordiality. 'I apologise if I'm interrupting.'

'Not at all,' she replied and led me into the front room.

In the parlour, furnished sedately with writing table and chairs, Reverend Tait sat writing with a dip-pen and ink near the glow of a lamp. As we entered the room, he set the pen on the inkstand, blotted his work and rose to his feet, brushing his lively hair back from his forehead. 'This is an unexpected pleasure,' he said as he greeted me and pulled a chair forward. Catherine resumed her seat nearby.

I removed my cap and fussed with my hair, now uncertain what to say.

'How is Mister Jamieson?' Reverend Tait asked, leaning back in his chair.

My gaze slid to the small window that overlooked the garden. 'I don't know.' Hallam and Catherine glanced at one another then back at me, a quizzical expression on their faces. 'Honestly, I truly don't know. His wounds have healed, but I fear he is deteriorating before my eyes.'

Hallam, Reverend Tait, seemed surprised. 'In what way?'

I groped for words. How might I tell of my troubles? 'His thought processes, his mind ... it's in disarray, he's

...' I let the sentence drift, hoping he would perceive my meaning and come to my aid.

He pursed his lips and steepled his fingers, an attitude he often assumed as if to focus his attention. 'I would expect you to be a fair judge of that,' he said.

'I'm no longer certain. My mind plays tricks. It may be lack of sleep, but betimes I think there are beasties in my head, as in his.'

'Oh, my dear,' Catherine exclaimed and offered me her slender hand. I clasped it as a drowning man grasps for something solid and her warmth flowed into me.

Hallam drew his chair closer. 'Missus Jamieson, the Lord does not send a burden greater than one's capacity to bear it.' He stared fixedly at me and his expression bade me pay heed. He understood the weakness of mankind and took great care to guide his flock through troubled waters. 'You are young and strong, a healer of some skill. You are not one to succumb to phantoms.' Despite his words I doubted my strength and this must have been apparent to him, as he called upon me to have courage. 'God has given you talents. You will find a way to confront Thorold's devils. You will bring him comfort, and in doing so, find your own.'

I leaned forward, taut, feeling as if the tension within me could catapult me from my chair at any moment. 'But how? I scarce understand him.' My gaze shifted again to the window as if the answer to my question might be found out there. 'He speaks of things I know little or nothing about. He thinks he's aboard ship. I can't convince him otherwise.' I was embarrassed to feel my face crumple in distress and I spread my hands, entreating my spiritual guide to grasp the extent of my concern. 'He cries out with horrors both night and day. He is consumed by them. I am at my wit's end.'

Catherine rose and spoke to her husband. 'I'll make a pot of tea while you talk,' she said and left the room.

Hallam silently observed me, as if I might indeed jump up and ... do what? Was I so unpredictable? Had I indeed fallen victim to Thorold's condition? I needed to explain what was truly troubling me.

'If I may ask you, Reverend Tait, about something Thorold said?'

'Of course.'

'He said a man fell from the *Falcon's* main mast to the deck – fell and probably died. The man ... if he ... that is, if I ...' I broke off, ill at ease describing events that Thorold may have truthfully witnessed on board ship. I hesitated before asking the Reverend, 'Should his widow be informed?' I searched Hallam Tait's face, hoping to discern some form of direction. Seeing none, I went on. 'I mean ... can we rely on the things Thorold says as truth? How may I know?'

'Ah, I comprehend your dilemma,' he replied. He stood gazing through the window to the garden as he pondered for a long moment. I became aware of a clock ticking somewhere behind me, and found myself counting the blip of the pulse in my tightly-held wrist, willing it to slow and keep time with the tock of the clock. He faced

48

me with his hands behind his back, rhythmically flicking his coat tails as if he, too, heard the clock dripping time away.

'You want to know whether to accept as truth the words of a man who, for the moment at least, appears unable to make a distinction between reality and imaginings. Yes?' He raised his eyebrows and when I nodded, continued. 'You are speculating that should his utterance be true, it may prove to be significant to a grieving widow or, for that matter, to someone with a proper interest in pronouncing cause of death, for official purposes.' He looked directly at me allowing his sonorous tone of voice to impart the seriousness of the situation.

It began to dawn on me that there was more at stake than a widow's feelings. 'It would come to that?'

He remained by the window, maintaining a clear level of formality. 'In all likelihood, yes. Thorold, as the *Falcon's* sole survivor, is the only person who can relate what happened to the ship and its crew. We must hope that he can recover his reason sufficiently to be able to acquaint us with the facts, rationally and with conviction.'

I dropped my gaze to my lap and reflected silently for a moment. 'You don't suppose ...' I raised my eyes to gauge his reaction to my next words. 'Is it possible that he is making it up?'

'Consciously telling an untruth? To what purpose?'

'I don't know.'

'Personally, I doubt it, but one cannot discount the possibility without professing to know Thorold's mental condition.'

It seemed to me that I was no further advanced than when I arrived; in fact, I had been presented with additional issues. 'What should I do, Reverend? I am sorely troubled.'

'As I perceive it, you have no compelling evidence on which to act. You have only the words of a man whose mind has been sorely afflicted by all manner of dreadful experiences. For the moment I would counsel you to refrain from repeating what he said. For my part, I will give the matter some further consideration. In the meantime, perhaps we'll – ah, here's our tea, and welcome it is.' Hallam gestured to Catherine to set the cups down on the small side table.

Catherine passed a cup to me and asked as I took it, 'Inga, would you be willing to accept some assistance at home, perhaps an occasional hour or two? I would be happy to help, without obligation, to relieve you a little of your burden.'

'Oh, Catherine, Missus Tait. That is a considerate offer. But I'm mindful of your own needs. I could not impose on you.'

'Not at all. I'd be pleased to help. Shall we say, tomorrow? I will prepare a meal, do whatever is useful. It will free you for evening chores, relieve you of that, at least, for a short while.'

I was about to object but Hallam interposed, whisking my protestation away with a wave of his hand. 'Now, Inga, we won't hear of any objection. Catherine will be glad of the walk. She gets about comfortably, and could perhaps prepare a meal for the four of us. I believe the offer is a good one, not to be refused,' he remarked, encouraging both of us with his happy face.

Catherine agreed. 'Of course. We shall eat together.'

~~~~~

The following afternoon I was returning home after a brief absence when, as arranged, Catherine Tait visited our croft. So I was surprised to see her striding across the fields towards me. She appeared somewhat breathless and troubled.

'Inga! I am so glad to have found you. I called at your croft, as we agreed. But ...'

'Is anything wrong?'

'You could say that, in some small way. May I walk with you?'

We turned and made our way back towards the croft.

'As I said,' Catherine continued, 'I visited the croft and called out to announce my arrival so as not to surprise Thorold with my sudden presence.'

'And you found him morose, as has been his habit of late?'

'Indeed. I announced myself and said I had come from the Manse to prepare a meal. But oh, the croft was so silent, as if not a soul was at home, and I felt cold air chill my ankles.'

'Of course, Thorold was likely abed, not wishing to stir. That, too, is his habit.'

'Indeed. I approached the door to the sleeping quarters, not wishing to disturb Thorold if he had, at last, been able to sleep, and spoke in a lowered tone from the main room. I asked if he was alright and believe I heard a voice on the other side of the door mumble something, but could not determine what it was. Assuming it was Thorold, I asked what he was saying.'

'And did he respond?'

'Yes. He spoke, this time more distinctly, his voice tight, suggesting a high level of anxiety. He said, the thermometer is 20° below freezing and the frost – it's iced everything to a thickness of six inches.'

'Ah. I see.' My steps slowed as we crested the rise and began to walk down the slope towards the croft. Thorold must think himself aboard ship again. 'I hope you were not too disturbed by Thorold's strange mumblings,' I said.

Catherine glanced quickly at me. 'No,' she said, but seemed a little hesitant. 'I offered to get him a warm cup of tea and his next words made me better grasp his condition.'

'His next words?'

'Yes. His voice had a sharp edge to it, impatient, pessimistic. He said the cook couldn't light a fire. He said everything was wet, nothing would burn. Everything was wet, bunks, clothing, everything.'

'He is deluded, Catherine. He thinks himself ...'

'... on board ship. I see that now. I decided to brew a pot of tea in any case, and took it to him. He sat on the bed. Oh, Inga, he looked so disconsolate, his eyes wide and staring. His poor scarred fingers plucked continually at a knot of bedclothes on his lap, folding and unfolding the edges like a fan. His crutches lay on the floor.'

I noted a look of distaste pass swiftly over Catherine's face and recalled the stale clothing waiting to be washed, and the lack of fresh air in the ben, despite my attempts to freshen the room by burning rosemary and sugar together. I found myself colouring with embarrassment.

Catherine continued her tale, unmindful of my discomfiture. 'I said, here, Thorold, I've made some tea. And he looked straight past me, as if someone stood behind me. I checked, but nobody was there. It was an odd feeling, as if he could see an apparition. I handed him the mug and exhorted him to drink it. He drank lustily and spoke again, more clearly this time. He said we're on short allowance you know, half a pound of salted beef, and only a few pounds of bread a week. He seemed so lucid that it quite took me by surprise. I objected that was barely enough to sustain life. But he said the beef will last a few weeks. I must say, Inga, I could almost smell the sourness of the rank meat. Then he told me it was hung in the shrouds and they splashed it with sea water every day. He said it freezes and keeps well ... until it's all gone. The thought quite upset me. That's when I tried to gather my wits about me and excused myself. I said you would be home soon and I would prepare a meal for us to eat together.'

'I'm sorry to put you to this trouble, Catherine. I believe you ought to return to the manse and leave me to look after Thorold.'

'Not at all. Thorold didn't even know me. He asked when I had joined the crew. He wanted to know if I was from another ship. I felt disinclined to present him with any facts that warred with his perception, so in half-truth that I pray will be forgiven, I replied that I was the cook's mate, before I left the room. I am ready now to return with you and we shall prepare a meal together. That is, if you don't mind.'

I linked my arm through hers as we approached the croft door. 'How could I mind, Catherine? You are a true friend in need and it will be good to have company.'

CHAPTER FIVE – *A Drop of Physic*

At the close of the Sunday morning worship service, Reverend Tait shepherded the other parishioners from the chapel, then briefly touched my arm and murmured, 'Would you care to call at the Manse tomorrow? I need to discuss something with you.'

'I'm able to stay and talk with you now, if that would suit.'

The Reverend's face flushed and, as if it was choking him, he inserted a finger behind his collar and loosened its grip on his throat.

'I have carried out some discreet enquiries. If you could manage tomorrow ...' He allowed his sentence to drift and glanced awkwardly about. Stragglers from the service were standing nearby, gathering in small clusters, pursuing muted conversations. He looked uncomfortable.

I had a notion I knew the reason for his unease. 'Am I to assume then that the matter is of some consequence?'

Reverend Tait clearly did not wish to pursue the conversation at this juncture. 'In a word, yes,' he said and hurried away, leaving me on the path by the church gate.

I left the chapel grounds, not wanting to converse with others, and moved towards home. As I walked, I caught sight of Rhona Sinclair sprinting to join me. Rhona was obviously in a jolly frame of mind, her eyes shining. She was a joy to behold, full of youth and vigour, not a worry in the world. Missus Sinclair would have conveyed my message to the girl.

'May I assume from your giddy mood that your mother has told you of my request?'

'Oh, aye, Missus Jamieson. Thank you, Missus Jamieson.' Rhona's exuberance made her somewhat breathless.

I stopped walking to ask, 'You're willing to help me with my salves and potions again?'

'Oh, yes,' Rhona replied. 'Tomorrow if I may.' She skipped and whirled about me as we walked. 'Mother says Mister Jamieson is getting better.'

I was afraid I'd given Missus Sinclair my assurances a little prematurely. 'Indeed, he is, though only a little at a time, not altogether as quickly as I had hoped,' I said, as truthfully as I dared.

'It's like a miracle, wouldn't you say? Some of my friends, their fathers were on the *Falcon* and they didn't come home.' The child had no guile.

'That is so.'

'They're very sad. It makes me sad too.'

'One of your tender years ought not dwell on such sadness too long. It was God's will.'

'Missus Jamieson,' the girl appeared to hesitate a moment, then went on, 'my friends …' she looked up at me, 'well, they question God. Will He forgive them?'

I was startled. 'Forgive them for what?'

'They want to know why God saved Mister Jamieson, and none of the others who had families.'

I halted and stood in silence, uncertain how to respond to Rhona's question. The girl pressed me. 'Is Mister Jamieson an ungodly man?'

I was taken aback. I suspected Rhona was repeating something she'd heard from others. Who would say such a thing? I scrabbled for an answer to her question.

'Your mother would not allow you to visit, if she had any such thought.'

'Oh, it's not Mother. It's other folk. They say Mister Jamieson is mad.'

'Granted, it might seem so to some. It's pain that makes him cry out. I expect one day it will stop.'

'I hope so.'

'So do I.' I took the girl's hand in a friendly manner. 'You will come tomorrow morning then, bright and early?'

She agreed and allowed me then to concentrate on her promise and pray she could shut out her fears and help me with my physic.

~~~~~

Soon after sunup the next morning Rhona and I were busy grinding dried herbs and storing the fine material in brown glass jars. I smiled my pleasure at her quick responses to let her see how pleased I was to have her assistance.

'Phew! Hog's fat smells awful, Missus Jamieson.' Rhona held her nose, its short round tip pinched between her fingers.

I laughed. 'Aye, it does. But if you add herbs and heat it gently it becomes quite pleasing. You'll see.'

'How long do you heat it?' The cuffs of Rhona's sleeves barely reached her wrists and a ribbon held her long tawny hair in a top-knot away from her face.

'Until it breaks down to liquid and is well steeped with the herbs. Then I strain it through that cloth and pour it into pots to cool.'

'What will you use it for?'

I pointed to a group of pots nearby. 'This one, with comfrey, will ease the aches and pains of age. That one, with elder bark and horse clippings, will heal cuts and bruises.'

Rhona tried unsuccessfully to fold her hands inside her sleeves.

'When my father was poorly last winter, you gave him a mixture to make him well.'

'Aye, indeed I did.'

'He drank from the blacksmith's trough – the one the horseshoes are quenched in – but it didn't help. He was glad of your medicine.'

I smiled at Rhona's ingenuousness. The blacksmith's trough was an old remedy of first resort.

58

'Would you show me how to make that one, Missus Jamieson? I want to learn how.'

I saw my own wish to ease the burdens of others reflected in Rhona's earnestness. I took up a piece of burdock root from the work table. 'It needs only a little care and attention. I boil some of this root in a small pitcher of water for a few minutes, and a large spoonful twice a day will make a man's blood strong again. I always keep it on hand when there's sickness about.'

I finished stirring the hog's fat and was about to strain it before pouring it into waiting pots.

'Would you like to strain this for me?' Rhona's eyes danced with pleasure. 'Be careful not to burn yourself – it's hot.'

'Thank you, Missus Jamieson. I'll be careful,' and she slowly strained the hot liquid through cloth into another container.

'Would you like to fill the pots for me too?'

'Oh, aye,' Rhona replied eagerly and measured a quantity of the mixture into each waiting pot. 'Will many folk get sick this winter, do ye think?'

I passed some herbs to Rhona to grind between stones while I considered her question. 'I hope not.'

'If they do, you'll need lots of ointments and confusions ready to use.'

I smiled at the girl's misnomer. 'Aye, that is true.' I wiped my hands on my apron. 'Now we can seal these jars with wax and put them away for use in winter.' We toiled until it was time for the main meal, when she would return home.

'What will we do tomorrow, Missus Jamieson?'

'Oh, there's no shortage of things to do. I'll be watching for you, Rhona.'

As we moved towards the croft door, Thorold bellowed from within.

'Get away, get out! The rats are leaving!'

Rhona hesitated. I lightly motioned her onwards. 'Don't be concerned. He's probably having a nightmare. He often does just before he wakes. Off you go. I'll see you on the morrow.'

Rhona sped off on foot, her bright braids bouncing on her shoulders as she ran.

'It's a bad omen. Rats know when a ship is doomed.'

'Hush now,' I said as I moved to the ben end of the croft. 'There are no rats here.'

'Of course not. They've all left. They would rather take their chances on an ice floe, than stay aboard and perish.'

'Nobody's going to perish. You're safe at home.'

I let Thorold ramble while I bustled about, scrubbing the bench and heating the meal I'd prepared earlier in the day.

'Why don't you sit near the hob where it's warm?'

'The wheel! Who's at the helm? A man daren't turn his attention away for a moment without courting disaster.'

'Come, lean on me and I'll set you down by the fire.'

Thorold lashed out with his arm and the unexpected blow swept me off my feet. I lay stunned on the floor.

'Avast there! Go to your station!'

His face was filled with rage and he turned abruptly and left the room. I remained on the floor until my vision cleared and I regained control of my breathing. Slowly I came to my feet, quietly took a seat by the fire and wept while Thorold continued ranting in the next room, ordering the crew to their stations, barking out orders and reprimands until, eventually, I heard them no more.

~~~~~~

In the hours that followed, I was thankful that time passed rather more peaceably. I had told Rhona she need not come to help me every day, settling on three days a week, for I feared dampening her enthusiasm. In truth, I feared she may be frightened away. Whenever I was alone at home with Thorold and all was peaceable, I was accustomed to spin fleece. Spinning was a quiet occupation and I was glad of it. I was not needed at the Magnusson farm so, after completing the routine chores, I sat at my wheel with a combed and carded fleece in a basket beside me. I fed fleece onto the bobbin and, working the treadle, began to draw fibres from the rolag, working the thread onto the spindle. I soon reached a soothing rhythm that calmed me. Thorold had settled and I planned to call on Reverend Tait while Thorold slept. I allowed myself to relax and enjoy the feel of the fleece as it passed through my fingers and the softening touch of lanolin on my roughened hands. It was better than gutting herring and smelling eternally of fish. I planned to take the goods I had spun and knitted to the Martinmas Fair in the hope of selling them. But I would have spun fleece anyway, without looking to sell what I made, for the pleasure I gained and the rhythm that soothed my troubled soul.

By the time I knocked on the door of the manse later that day, I felt quite at ease. Reverend Tait opened the door. Catherine Tait was nowhere to be seen.

'Reverend Tait. I expected Catherine to come to the door.'

'She's calling on parishioners.' He ushered me into the front parlour and we seated ourselves in the overstuffed chairs that were arranged on one side of the room.

'I want to discuss Thorold's comment about the man who met his death on the *Falcon*, among other things.'

'Other things?'

Reverend Tait pursed his lips and fiddled with his clerical collar, easing it away from his throat. I noticed that he avoided meeting my eyes.

'I made enquiries in relation to the weight Thorold's words might carry, in a legal sense. And of the likely consequences of making them known, to the man's widow, for example.' He paused for a moment before continuing. 'Whilst undertaking these enquiries, through discreet sources, I chanced upon a disturbing rumour.'

'A rumour?'

'Yes. The fate of Thorold's shipmate is as nothing, alongside the gossip – that Thorold is insane and in Satan's power, and that you are his handmaiden, bent on spreading disbelief through the community.'

I felt the skin on my face shrink and tighten. Who would spread such mischief abroad? What damage might this do to Thorold's recovery and to my own wellbeing? My hands were cold and clammy and I clasped them firmly together to prevent them from trembling.

Reverend Tait leaned forward. 'I'm sorry to tell you this.'

I drew away and leaned back in the chair, feeling my body stiffen as if to guard against a blow. 'May I have a glass of water, please?'

'Of course.' He left the room, allowing me time to collect myself before he returned, tumbler in hand.

'Here.' He handed me the water and sat quietly while I sipped.

'Where did you hear this talk?'

'That's not important.'

'It is to me. What is your opinion of what people are saying?'

'My opinion?' His gaze was now direct, unflinching. 'I believe Satan works His evil ways through us, but Thorold's struggle is corporeal, a consequence of terrible experiences, not of moral turpitude. We must pray that eventually the nightmares and aggression will diminish and his health will return.'

'And me? Do you believe I do the Devil's work?'

'No, I do not. I have seen you work for the good of others.'

I held back the tears that were threatening to overtake me.

'Your struggles are not born of the Devil, though a lesser person might have turned away from God after such losses as you've suffered. You have not turned away from the Lord, have you?'

'Of course not. Why would people speak of me so? What have I done? Who would do this to me?' I bunched my handkerchief in my hand.

'Gossip such as this arises from superstition and fear, not from anything tangible.'

'I have no means, no weapon to combat this.' I felt as though my insides had been ripped out of me, gutted like a herring. Had I not lost enough? Was I destined to lose my reputation as well?

He stood and looked across the garden beyond the church facade, as if searching the pallid skies for reassurance. 'If you reveal Thorold's story of the man's fate it will give substance for the gossips to focus on. You and Thorold will suffer serious consequences. Again, I must counsel you against it, at least until the rumours abate.'

'So. Thorold and I are to keep our counsel, remain isolated in our troubles. And the widow and her family are to continue wondering what happened to their husband and father while we keep the knowledge to ourselves.' I felt besieged, and then, unexpectedly, anger began surging in my chest and astonished me with its energy. I was swept into a net that was not of my own making and desperately wanted to break free.

'For the moment. You need to protect yourself and Thorold.'

'And you? What will you do? You are privy to the same knowledge as I.'

'I am not the one under condemnation. But I will watch and pray on your behalf.'

The room seemed suddenly very small and unbearably stuffy. I had to get outside, get away. I had no champion who might do battle for me.

'I'll call on you in a few days,' he said.

'I'd prefer you didn't, Reverend. Give my regards to Missus Tait.' I was aware how abrupt I sounded, but I needed to be alone and fled the house without observing formalities.

~~~~~

The following day, I closeted myself in the croft, tending to Thorold's needs and working to put up a batch of herbal remedies, ready for the coming winter months when illness usually struck the Islands. A sense of wretchedness led me to shrink from contact with others. I was becoming withdrawn, like Thorold, as a result of my disappointment and anger at the gossip that was abroad. My mind was concentrated on preparing oils and potions and at first I did not hear the knock on the door. It was tentative to begin with, then became louder until it penetrated my consciousness. At the door, Rhona stood jigging about, her agitation apparent.

'Missus Jamieson, come quickly. Father is sick again. Mother says he needs your special remedy.'

Urged by Rhona's anxiety and glad of the distraction, I snatched up my basket, added a few supplies and made haste to the Sinclair croft. Marian stood waiting at the door and bade me enter. In hurried tones, she acquainted me with Harald's trouble as she led me to his sickbed at the furthest end of the croft. The space was crammed with beds and clothing and there was barely room to move. The cloying miasma of sickness filled the air in the small room.

'He has a fever and his legs cramp until he cries out. He's emptied himself of everything he's eaten over the last week. It spews from both ends, and he eats no food.'

I felt the tension in the house. This was different from Harald's previous troubles. It reminded me of the loss of my dear sister and guide years earlier, from a condition nobody could cure. I desperately hoped that same dreaded malady would not visit the community again. We lost so many people then in a few brief weeks and the pain of so much loss was unbearable. I prayed the Lord it would not happen again.

'Water and blankets,' I instructed Marian. 'I need both.'

Seeing Harald, I wondered how he was still with us. His body appeared deflated, as if drained of all life, the skin clinging to his bones like so much dried parchment.

His eyes were sunken into great hollows in his face, his breath was fetid and he lay limp on the bed. The sharp stench of urine was heavy in the room. I did my best to ignore it while I tried to decide how to help the man struggling with sickness.

Marian reappeared with a pan of water and a thick quilt. 'Spread the quilt over him,' I said. 'He needs to keep warm, despite the fever.' The two of us settled Harald as much as possible and I wiped perspiration from his brow. 'Now let's give him a sip of water and see if he keeps it down.'

Harald needed support to sip from the beaker and no sooner had he done so than he vomited. His gut-wrenching rejection of any sustenance worried me. It was not a good sign. After Marian cleaned the mess, I beckoned her to the hearth in the next room.

'I want you to give Harald a large spoonful of ginger tea every couple of hours. I know he may not be able to keep it down, but keep trying. Just a sip or two at first and increase the amount when you can. It will help settle his bowels. It's as well I prepared some from fresh hawthorn only this week and I think an infusion of it might stop the vomiting. Give it to him three times a day. I also want you to rub this on his legs at night.' I handed her a pot. 'It's made from yarrow and will help with the cramps.'

Marian looked ready to weep. 'Oh, thank you, Missus Jamieson. I'm in your debt.'

I attempted to reassure the woman. 'Let me know how he is tomorrow. Send Rhona to fetch more if you need it.'

I took my leave and was glad of the fresh air outside the croft, the salt-tanged stiff breeze that carried the smell of sickness away.

~~~~~

Early the next morning I received a visit from Lillian Isbister, Robbie Isbister's widow. She was loath to come indoors but it was soon apparent she was in need of my physic.

'Missus Jamieson. Ellen is poorly and I am at my wit's end to know what to do. She has a fever and ...'

'She vomits?'

'Aye and runs to the pot as well.'

'Come in and I will get some preparations for you.' I led her indoors and sat her at my table while I gathered the remedies together. It sounded much as Harald Sinclair was suffering, but I prayed it was not.

'Give the child a few sips of ginger tea to help settle her stomach. And keep her warm, despite her fever.'

'It will be hard with her brothers dashing in and out.'

'Fresh air should do no harm, providing she is not chilled. With good fortune, whatever it is that ails her will wane.'

'Thank you, Missus Jamieson.' She paid me for my help and left quietly.

'Let me know how she is in a day or two, Lillian,' I called as she turned for home.

I was soon to receive another visitor. Within hours Rhona was again at my door and this time her expression was crestfallen.

'Rhona. How is your father?'

'Not good, Missus Jamieson. Mother is doing her best, but he keeps messing and ...' She wrinkled her nose. The girl appeared close to tears. 'He's really sick, isn't he?' It wasn't a question. She knew the answer.

'Aye, child. Your father is very ill. But we'll do what we can to help him. Does your mother need more of the things I left yesterday?'

Rhona seemed disconcerted. 'No, thank you. She says will you come and look at father again. She says is there anything else you can do?'

I felt my stomach clench but stayed calm in an effort to reassure Rhona. 'Today I'll prepare something else that might help. But tell your mother to keep trying with the things I gave her for at least another day. It is too early to expect much improvement.'

'But you said ... you asked her to let you know how he is.' Rhona was anxious, trying to understand.

'Aye, that is true. But I need to give each remedy a chance to work for a day or two. That's how I can tell which remedy works best. So I check on him each day to know when he starts to get better.'

'I see.' The explanation appeared to satisfy the girl.

'Wait at least another day, then let me know how he is. Will you do that for me?'

'Aye, Missus Jamieson. Thank you, Missus Jamieson.' And Rhona turned towards home.

I stood at the door of the croft and watched the girl as she headed down the hill. Rhona appeared reassured, but I was worried. My physic ought to have made a difference in a little more than a day. If Harald Sinclair was no better, he was deeply ill and I feared what I might have to face in the coming days. I was concerned enough to visit Lillian Isbister at home and enquire after her daughter.

'Ellen is much improved, Missus Jamieson. I am much obliged for your help. She is taking small amounts of soft food and her fever is less.'

'I am pleased to hear she is faring better,' I said and was truly thankful. 'Keep giving her the ginger tea. It will help to wash the sickness from her system,' I said and returned home with greater lightness of spirit.

~~~~~~

Yet I had cause to worry. It seemed only a matter of hours before Harald Sinclair's condition seriously declined and within another day he went to his eternal rest. And he was only the first among many who contracted the illness and left grieving families. However much I wished otherwise, the illness continued to assail the community and I despaired of finding a solution to ease people's ills. This was an entirely new experience, facing an unknown condition that I could not heal or treat. Ellen Isbister was one of the few who recovered from the sickness and for that I was grateful. Yet there were so many others who continued to fall victim to the malady. A few unhappy creatures went to clootie wells and soaked cloths in the water, dabbing those who were suffering in the hope of transferring some good fortune, before tying the cloths to the well. But it was all to no avail.

My ministrations were eagerly sought and the meagre supplies of herbal remedies that I had prepared for the oncoming winter soon proved insufficient to meet the needs of the sufferers, many of whom succumbed to the mysterious condition. The pity of it was that the elderly, the sickly and the newborns were not the only victims: previously hale and hearty menfolk were passing as often as those already frail. There seemed no reason why some should die and others survive and while my physic appeared to be help in some instances it was not so in others. It was a mystery illness with no obvious solution. I did what I could, even, in my desperation, resorting to the use of cramp bone amulets from the knuckles of sheep, something I shrank from as a useless superstition that had never, to my knowledge, proved helpful. It was a desperate measure and I expected nothing by using them, and my lack of confidence in the amulets proved to be well placed.

If only I could know the cause of this malady. Perhaps it did not come from the stomach as I thought. Perhaps I ought to treat it with some other physic – but what? I paced and surveyed my dwindling supplies. We had so little on the Islands that I could harvest for remedies at this time of year. Perhaps I might send to the south for remedies that may be found on the Scottish mainland. But then I frowned, not certain that my knowledge would extend to identifying and locating the right ingredients. Night after night, exhausted after tending to Thorold as well as those who asked my help, I dredged from my memory obscure herbal recipes my mother had used years before, when she dealt with a malady that took the lives of many in the district.

Back then my mother, bless her heart, had agonised over her inability to save Mary, for she was herself a healer. Everyone relied on her knowledge and skill, yet she had been helpless to save her own kin. I was appalled to see my mother's rich brown hair swiftly blanch to white as she wailed for her first-born daughter.

'I must hae done wrong. I should hae been able to heal our bairn.'

'Ye're no at fault,' father told her but mother had wrung her hands and wept.

'Ah, but I am. I know and the Lord knows – I failed her.'

'Come now, mother. You couldna do more.' Father had put his arm around mother's trembling shoulders, discounting his own grief in an effort to comfort her.

'I'll no' make remedies again.'

'Wheesht now, woman. What are ye saying?'

'I'm no' going to do it. It's no good if I can't save my ain child.' Her eyes were red with weeping, bottomless pools of sorrow.

'What are ye saying? We've Jacob and Inga and Charlotte with us still.'

Mother had risen from her chair and stood stiff and formal. 'I've spoken. I'll no' do it again.'

My heart had ached and propelled me to fill the breach. 'Mother. Teach me. I can do it; I can make the mixtures.'

Mother had halted on her way out of the room and turned to me, the elder of her remaining daughters, for Charlotte was three years my junior. I remember feeling all the hope a sixteen-year-old could command, wanting mother to see my sincerity and, indeed, my own distress in the pleading I made.

'You, child?' she had said, softly.

'Aye. Show me, mother.'

She had hesitated until she saw father take my hand, willing her to consider my proposition. Mother's gaze softened. 'Inga, my wee hen.' And I was elated with dreams of the future as she relinquished the role of healer to me, a role I had relished, until now, when I was faced with the same challenge that my mother faced before me. It wasn't the first time the Islands had been so afflicted yet nobody knew from whence the illness came, not even Doctor Anderson. He also lost many patients from the towns and surrounding communities and struggled to find an answer. Everyone was suffering.

~~~~~

One afternoon, while I was busy trying to brew a batch of remedies, there came a knock at the door. It was Charlotte.

'Could you use some help, Inga?'

'Do come in, Charlotte. As you see, I am trying to find a remedy for the illness that has struck this place. Do you remember mother working with her pots and potions?'

'Aye, I do. I was only a young 'un then, but I recall her sorrow when Mary was struck with the fever. She tried but ...'

'Yes. I miss Mary, too.' With the passage of time, it was becoming more difficult to remember dear Mary's face. 'Do you recall anything of mother's mixtures?'

'Not at all. Though I might have liked brewing things and putting the mixture in pots, as she did. But I was too young.'

'Not at all. Young Rhona who helps me occasionally, she is about the same age as you were when Mary died, in fact a wee bit younger. And she learns quickly, as you might have if you had joined mother and me in herbals.'

'Well, I am here now, so let us begin.'

We worked side by side and talked.

'I believe you spend a good deal of time with Mister Gifford and his bairns. What does father say of your service there?'

Charlotte laughed. 'Father takes no heed of my comings and goings. It is Jacob who scolds me and Norah who counsels against being thought forward.'

'And are you ... forward I mean?'

She had the grace to blush. 'I have had an interest in Mister Gifford for some time, since I first became aware of him.' She glanced at me, then away at the pots she was filling. 'He needs help with the young ones, with his wife gone these two years past.' She smiled. 'They are a handful, boisterous and fun and their care is a service I am glad to give.'

'And have you set your cap at Mister Gifford then, Charlotte?'

'If he would have me.'

'Has he given any indication of his feelings?'

She turned and looked directly at me. 'Why, yes. In fact, he took me by the hand and we went walking with the bairns not more than two days ago. He asked me then if I would consider his hand in marriage.'

'And you would?'

'I said yes.' She grinned at me, looking as mischievous as any child.

'And he has presented himself to father and to Jacob?'

'Yes, and they approve.'

'Good. You have chosen well, Charlotte. I am glad for you.'

She threw her arms around me and we hugged one another. 'I am so glad you approve,' she said. 'It is important that you do.'

'Yes, I do approve. He is an upright young man with a good heart and you will make a bonny wife and mother.'

'We are to be wed in the new year, in January. Will you be my witness?'

'Of course I will. It would give me the greatest pleasure.'

We worked happily together and, in the few hours she had available, we put up a goodly range of remedies, although our sisterly confidences were uppermost in both our minds. Charlotte's presence gladdened my heart. I had longed for her company and to have my young sister at my side, working together on infusions and decoctions, was a joy. To hear her speak of her feelings for Mister Gifford was an added pleasure and I was doubly pleased at her betrothal.

'I will make myself available again, should you need me,' Charlotte said as the time came for her to leave.

'You are welcome any time, dear sister, but I expect you will be busy with other chores from now on,' I said. 'You have a wedding to plan and there will be many calls on your time. God bless you, my darling girl,' I said and it warmed my heart to see her bounce across the fields.

~~~~~~

Then, one day, nobody came to our door. I had an entire day uninterrupted to spend at home tending to chores and caring for Thorold whose dark moods left him brooding by the peat fire I set each morning in the hearth. I did not question why we were left uninterrupted, assuming each was tending his own in places of sickness all over the Islands. I tried to relax and take some meagre pleasure in familiar routines. I even jollied Thorold to turn his hand to whittling.

'You've two good hands, my dear,' I told him. 'You've no need for feet to make something useful we can sell.' For once, Thorold agreed and asked that I fetch something he could work with.

It was when I walked to the trader's to buy a knife for him that I became aware of a subtle change. At first, I thought there were fewer people about because of the level of mourning in the community. Then I saw some ladies from the parish hurry into a neighbour's house and shut the door as if wishing not to be seen. Soon after, a group of bairns were hurriedly called indoors, and a man walking towards me abruptly changed direction and retraced his footsteps.

People seemed to appear and disappear so swiftly, they might be wraiths flitting between headstones in the churchyard. Surely it was the illness producing this effect and disturbing my mind. And then, I remembered Mister Tully putting down the knife I had bought and, rather than taking my coins, suggesting I leave the money there for him to deal with later, as he had his hands full at the moment. I remembered him quickly lifting a sack of flour and hurrying off as I made my way outside. Could it be that perhaps people were afraid of me? Did they imagine I carried the malady with me, that I was responsible for spreading the disease? I was aghast at the thought but rapidly convinced myself of the proposition.

I was being spurned by my neighbours; I was confounded and felt fear myself. If people were turning away from me, what could I do to reassure them? Could I reassure them? Were they right to keep their distance from me? After all, I had visited the homes of everyone who was sick. Yet I was not ill, neither was Thorold, just as Rhona had said. The dread and guilt that overcame me when my sister Mary fell victim to disease, leaving me whole, made itself felt once more. I was overcome with the need to talk to someone I could trust. Reverend Tait would know how I might respond to this new challenge. When I needed someone to guide me, his voice alone could soothe my troubled spirit. I changed direction and moved towards the Manse.

CHAPTER SIX – *Superstition*

When I arrived, I found Hallam poring over scriptures while Catherine was busy scrubbing the deal table in the kitchen.

'Come in and take a seat,' Hallam said as he ushered me into the front parlour and gestured to a fireside chair. 'It's fresh outside and warm in here. Now ... how may I be of assistance?' Hallam appeared in a cheerful frame of mind.

'I'm beset with fears and worries and I need your advice.'

At my words, Hallam's face assumed a serious expression. 'Certainly.'

At first I held my basket close on my lap and focused on its contents. Then, aware that Hallam was waiting to be informed of my troubles, I lifted my face and began. 'I am come to the belief that people are afraid of me.'

Reverend Tait exclaimed, 'Afraid? Of you?' as if it could not be. Then he asked, 'But why? What is it that leads you to believe such a thing?'

I twisted my hands together and fidgeted with my basket as I spoke, jigging my knees up and down in my nervousness. 'I had an errand and Mister Tully ... he ... well, he avoided any contact with me or anything I handled. And there were ladies who scuttled indoors as if shunning a beggar ... and quickly called their bairns to their sides, and ...' I hesitated before continuing. 'A man who was clearly walking towards me, turned and walked back the way he had come.' It pained me to speak these thoughts aloud and I quickly dropped my gaze to my lap to avoid seeing Hallam's expression. 'Why would they do that if they were not afraid of me, afraid I carry the sickness with me?' I was near to weeping. 'They see me as they might the Devil's handmaiden, as rumour has it.'

'Ah, I see.' Hallam drew his chair a fraction closer, then folded his hands on his knees. 'You may well think their actions suggest fear of the sickness but everyone feels that fear at this time. There is nothing remarkable in that. And had you considered there might be legitimate reason for their actions, reason that has naught to do with you?'

'What other reason might they have?'

In my eagerness I raised my head and saw Hallam run one hand through his unruly hair, take a handkerchief from his vest pocket and wipe his hands. 'Well, the trader may well have had urgent tasks to attend to. The ladies, well, they frequently have need to rush indoors to attend to chores, and perhaps the bairns had already been scolded for playing outdoors on such a bitter day.'

'And the man?'

'Could he not have recalled something he needed to fetch and turned to pursue that purpose? Had you not thought of that?'

My shoulders slumped and I felt my breath release, unaware of how much tension I had been restraining. 'Aye, of course. That is reasonable. You must think me addle-brained.'

Hallam rose from his chair and I did likewise. 'You are surely feeling the strain of recent events, and Thorold's ramblings are beginning to transmit their unease to you.' He guided me gently towards the front door.

'Thank you, Reverend. I rely on you for good counsel.'

'Have a care to your own health, Missus Jamieson. We all have need of you in these trying times. Missus Isbister has told me of your healing touch with young Ellen.'

I felt his warm and gentle hand on my back and when we reached the door, without intent, I grasped his hands in an excess of gratitude and need and held them, noting that he did not shrink from my touch. Then my face flamed with colour and I saw a twinning tint rise from beneath Hallam's clerical collar. I swiftly disengaged and left, fearing I had transgressed in a most unseemly manner.

~~~~

At home my embarrassment began to leave me, but it returned of a sudden when Catherine Tait knocked on our door. I gathered myself and tried to overcome my lack of ease, intent on good manners.

'Missus Tait, do come in.'

'Catherine, please. Don't let us fall on formality between us.'

'Thank you, Catherine.' Did she not notice and wonder at my nervousness?

'I am sorry to have missed your visit to my dear husband. And how is Thorold today? Improving I would hope.'

'Not improving, but he's no worse and for that I am grateful.'

We stepped into the living space and Catherine greeted Thorold who sat whittling beside the peat fire.

'What is that you are making?' Catherine stepped closer to see the object that was taking shape in Thorold's hands. He immediately tucked it out of sight under the folds of his overshirt.

'Nothing of interest to you,' he said and stared into the glow from the burning peat.

Catherine appeared to accept, or at least tolerate, Thorold's brusqueness and I hurried to fill the breach of etiquette, politely offering our guest a chair. The exchange had afforded me an opportunity to settle myself.

'I came to ask you, Inga, if could you provide me with remedies, as Hallam and I have both been suffering some mild fever and coughs. You may have a headache remedy as well, to help us strengthen ourselves against the winter chills that daily seep into our bones.' She shivered involuntarily and drew her shawl close around her shoulders.

I bade her sit beside the fire.   'I can make a pot of warming tea for you now, if you please. It will refresh you a little.'

'That would be kind of you, my dear. Thank you.'

I spooned some of the mix into a pot and poured hot water over it, setting it aside to brew while I reached for my yarrow preparation.   'An infusion of this, several times a day, will help against the fever and coughs. And a pot of tea from these dried herbs will ease your head.'   I handed the remedies to Catherine and attended to the tea.

'How is your young helper faring?' Catherine asked. 'I hear she is keen to learn the healing arts from you.'

I set beakers on the table. 'Rhona is an apt pupil and takes in knowledge quickly.   I am pleased to have her company and her assistance.'

'With all the sickness about and the demands on your time, I'm sure Rhona must be a great help.'

'That she is.   It frees me to tend to Thorold's needs, although he is becoming more independent as he moves about a little better with the aid of sticks.'

Mention of his name prompted Thorold to rise from his seat, take the sticks that were propped nearby and move to the ben end, shutting the door noisily behind him. Catherine and I glanced a moment at the door, then resumed talking.

'Your husband appears more settled, Inga. In truth, is he no better?'

'Indeed, any improvement is so small as to be barely noticeable. His silences speak more of his distress. And at night ....'

'He remains restless?'

'Indeed.' I poured the tea. 'I resort to herbals to ease my own headache. Thorold's murmurings interrupt our sleep night after night and there are days when I find it difficult to go about my chores.'

'Have you asked him about his distress, what it is that ails him?

'A number of times, but he has no wish to speak of it, even in daylight hours. It is only at night ... and then his speech is ... gruff, scrambled if you will. I can barely interpret what he says.' We sipped our tea. 'I worry about the future, Catherine. I fear what is to become of us. This is not the life I imagined when we wed.'

Catherine finished her tea and set her cup down. 'None of us know what the future holds. All I know is we must rely on the good Lord for our strength and support. I believe He does not test us beyond our forbearance.'

'I am uncertain about my faith in recent times. All the death and misery that has been visited upon us makes me wonder if He watches over us still. Why would He inflict such suffering on families? What have we done to deserve the burdens He places on our shoulders? Are we so wicked that He turns His back on us?'

Catherine reached forward and took my hands between her own. 'Many have asked these questions before us and many will again. It is for us to pray and have faith. That is what faith is all about, my dear. Trust in God and He will be your guide.'

I remained silent.

'Inga, my friend, those who are left are spared by God to fulfil His purpose on this earth. You, my dear, are one of those people and must trust Him to show you the way.'

'Catherine ...'

'Take no account of village gossip.'

'So, you've heard it too.'

'Yes. And I am quick to counter it, as you should be. I know you work hard and deeply feel the pain of those who suffer. It is their fear and grief that leads them astray, as we all stray from time to time, like the Lord's wandering sheep. They will come to see the error of their ways, you'll see.'

My thanks were warm as Catherine rose and took her leave. I sighed and reflected on the war within me. Was my trespass, warming my heart at Hallam's expense, a momentary aberration that might so easily be forgiven?

My confidence lifted, I felt ready to face the morrow and decided to visit my father's property next day and help with the family chores, as I once did before Thorold returned from the Arctic. Now that he was healing and needed my presence less, it would do my spirits good to return to some semblance of the routine I missed. And now that Charlotte was betrothed and wedding plans were occupying her time, my labour would be welcome.

~~~~~

The Magnusson acreage lay at a distance from our croft. In the blustery conditions, it took me more than an hour to make my way on foot where I was greeted by loud cries of 'Aunt Inga! Aunt Inga!'

'Quiet, bairns,' echoed from the house. Norah emerged wiping floury hands on her apron. 'Hello Inga, come inside. It's good to see you. How is Thorold?'

'Improving, I believe, but slowly.'

'To what do we owe this visit? We've seen nothing of you for many days.'

'I am of a mind to help father and Jacob with the chores today. With Charlotte otherwise occupied, I stand ready to help.'

'My, that sounds promising. But don't you have your hands full, with Thorold and ... remedies and ... everything?'

I noticed the hesitation and saw that Norah had returned to kneading the dough, without looking at me. 'Aye. My days are well taken up with chores and people continue to seek my help. But I thought I'd ask ...'

'Ask what?' came a gruff voice from the doorway. Jacob appeared, clad in sweat-sodden work clothes, his hands grimy from the outdoors. 'What is it you come for?'

Surprised by his rough tone, I became aware of my father standing behind my brother, both men watching me with closed expressions.

'I come to offer my assistance. I am free to do chores here today, if you are agreeable.'

86

'Free, is it you are? And your Devil's work? Have you none of that to do?' Jacob stood unmoving in the doorway.

'Outside, bairns!' Norah commanded the two small girls, who willingly ran outside to play.

'Devil's work? Whatever do you mean?'

'Your dealings with the spirit world, that's what I mean.'

I felt blood rush to my head in the face of Jacob's attack. 'I have no dealings with the spirit world. Nor with the Devil. And do you have the gall to say I do?'

'Aye, that I do. It is widely known what you do.'

'By whom is it widely known? By you and your big mouth and busy tongue?'

'Well might you try to blame others. But it is by your own hands it is known. You cannot deny you have used bone amulets to deal with the sickness. You have used clootie cloths and ...'

'I have not!'

'We've heard it from many at morning chapel. Our dear mother would never have stooped so low as to deal with the spirits from the other world. I'll not have one who does the Devil's work in this house!' Jacob snarled and raised his hand, poking me in the shoulder as he spoke. 'You are to blame for the cattle blight; you are bringing this place undone. After all the work I have put into giving this family a future, you are cursing the very ground we stand on.'

Heat flooded my innards and I felt it rising to choke me, despite the chill in the air. Now I knew where the gossip had begun.

Jacob went on. 'We wonder, why do folk die all around us, yet you and Thorold remain whole? You who entered the homes and tended every one of those sick people, yet are well. You, who would turn a bairn into a Devil worshipper. You ....'

'I'll not hear another word of this.' I shouted at Jacob. 'Now I know who I have to thank for the gossip that's been put abroad in this place. You are a serpent, a betrayer of your own kind. And you, father? What of you?' I turned hot eyes on my father who had remained silent. 'Do you believe I deal with the spirits, with the Devil's work?'

Father looked at the floor and made tocking noises as he had years ago when, as young bairns, we had misbehaved. 'Mother would not have dealt so. I trusted you not to make contact with the other side.'

'I shan't set foot in this house again until you take back what's been said today,' I told them, barely controlling the anger that fought to erupt. My voice sounded sour and threatening, even to me, as I looked at each of them in turn. 'Even you, Norah. And I thought you a friend.'

'We don't want you here to blight our cattle and our crops. Best you be gone, witch,' Jacob spat at me.

'Witch is it now? I thank the Lord there are those who remain unblinkered.'

'Well you may. It is those with clear sight who see what you have become,' he shouted after me as I ran home. Was it come to this now, even my own kin turned against me? What had I done to bring about such disfavour? Every step of the way I went over in my mind all that had been said, realising as I did that Jacob's word held standing in the community and his gossip would work to destroy my reputation as an honest, God-fearing woman.

~~~~~~

It was mid-November and the weather turned bleak. Constant rain created rivulets that ran down the sides of hills and into nooks and crannies in crofts and barns. Mud was underfoot everywhere and the wind that carried the rain over the fields felt like fingers of ice searching for a grasp of every aching joint. Thorold felt the pain in his bones, where once he had a sound footing, and my remedies eased his discomfort only briefly. While the wet weather made it easier to turn the clods of earth for the graves of those newly departed, it made ordinary life miserable for those who remained. People stayed indoors and added extra layers of clothing that would not be shed until the warmth of spring arrived.

Confined to the cramped space I occupied with Thorold, my world shrank around me. I now knew the source of the rumours that spread about me, rumours that caused Rhona to question her loyalty, rumours that urged people in the village to hurry indoors when I passed. But I had no weapons with which to fight the gossip, other than my tremulous faith and the quiet support of Reverend Hallam Tait and his wife, Catherine. But the full extent of my troubles did not become apparent until the Martinmas Fair at the end of the month.

The day of the Fair dawned crisp and clear after a night of rain. All over the Islands people scurried about preparing for a day of trade and socialising. They erected tents, set up trestles, and displayed their goods and livestock.

'Come, Thorold, it will do you good to get out into the fresh air. People will be anxious to shake your hand and wish you well.' He looked horrified. What had I said that was so awful?

'Thorold? Will you come with me?'

'No. They'll like as not want to hang me, not shake my hand.'

'Why would anyone want to hang you? Please, Thorold. It is going to be a rousing Fair with a lot to do. Please, come along and help me.'

He stood up abruptly and banged the table with bunched fists.

'No, I said. You heard me.'

'But Thorold ...'

'Begone, woman. Just go!'

His anger alarmed me. I could not understand where it came from, but I had no wish to stir it further. So I collected my goods and bundled them into a barrow and pushed it over the fields towards the Fair. It was as well that I laboured alone to get to the grounds and set up my stall. I had a lot to occupy my mind and barely noticed my neighbours busy arranging their own wares. Together with the stallholders, there were many others drawn by the chance to buy sound home-made goods for the coming season, goods that surpassed those sold by the wandering tinkers. Everywhere around me people were exchanging cheerful greetings with friends, neighbours and strangers alike. It promised to be a bonny day.

Martinmas was a time when farmers hired labour for the coming year. Many hopefuls trudged around in the wet grass looking for gainful employment, but only a few farmers had the wherewithal to hire extra help. The sickness and cost of interments, to those who had suffered bereavement, dealt a blow to families struggling to feed themselves and pay bills.

At least the herring fishermen attracted a good deal of custom and were able to sell most of their surplus catch. Cries of 'Fresh herrings here!' could be heard across the grounds. Crofts everywhere would reek for days of herring being smoked over hearths. Likewise, abundant supplies of wool were on display, particularly this year, as Mister Standen, who took much of the island knitwear for sale on the British mainland, had himself collapsed and died mid-year of pneumonia, leaving his business interests in the hands of family who had not yet taken it up again.

'I see you've knitted woollens, Missus Jamieson,' a familiar voice announced itself to me.

'Why, yes, Missus Isbister, I have.'

''Tis a pity about poor Mister Standen. He'll be missed by us hereabouts.'

'Indeed. We have sore need of a merchant for our woollens.'

'There's an opportunity for one of our ain folk to raise himself up,' Lillian said.

'Maybe so. It would bear some consideration.'

'That would be a fine thing,' she said and wandered away. She was the first and last person to stop and pass the time of day with me. Other exchanges were not pleasantries but wholly commercial.

As the day wore on I managed to sell all the skeins of wool I'd spun, but only one knitted fisherman's pullover and none of the fine lace shawls I had on hand. Granted, a lot of folk were finding it difficult to spare the money, so I lowered the price of the garments, even offered to trade them for something else that might be offered rather than cash, but still they went begging for a buyer. The shawls appeared less suited to the gentlefolk of the Shetlands than they were to the people of Edinburgh or London. Perhaps Mister Standen's business was of more interest to a Londoner than an Islander.

Early in the afternoon, I saw Jacob and Norah and the bairns buying items from nearby stalls. Charlotte and Laurence walked with them. Charlotte saw me and waved, appearing intent on approaching me, but Jacob noticed and I heard him scold her: 'We will none of us speak to that woman. You will stay with us.'

92

Laurence appeared disconcerted by this sudden pronouncement and frowned at Jacob. But despite Charlotte's clear wish to speak with me, Jacob insisted that they move away, ignoring Charlotte's entreaties and Laurence's polite enquiry. It saddened me, but there was nothing I could do.

I had set out a selection of items Thorold had whittled, hoping to supplement our earnings from his efforts, yet folk paid little heed; only the children seemed interested. I was disheartened by my lack of success and loath to let Thorold know that his whittling was not sought. I determined to give the pieces away if they could not be sold, simply to encourage his activity. Better days might come upon us next year but our meagre earnings did not augur well for that hope.

By the time the Fair ended and people began to make their way home, my pockets were not strained and I knew that I was being shunned in the bluntest way. I trudged homewards with a heavy sense of foreboding, but tried not to allow room to my disappointment and fears, lest it provoke another of Thorold's rages.

CHAPTER SEVEN – *The Devil's Work*

At home, Thorold's night-time ramblings increased in intensity as the spectre of winter closed its dark drapes around us. Whatever misfortune befell those aboard the *Falcon*, only Thorold knew and his torture knew no bounds, spreading over both of us like a shroud, smothering any vision of a bright future. The only joy in my life was the vision of the northern lights as they rolled across the winter skies. When I saw their green glow I stood outside and let the colour and movement wash over me as if a fairy curtain was wafting away my cares.

Yet, as each day broke, grey and cold, the sun hardly dared to light the landscape and with every darkening day I became more convinced that Thorold had descended into madness and would drag me with him. On occasion he failed to recognise me, addressing me as 'Cook' or 'Bos'n'. Gentle Catherine Tait came regularly to lend assistance and soothe me in the midst of my isolation. Yet even Catherine could not banish the ghosts that tore at the bonds Thorold and I had barely begun to weave.

'What am I to do?' I implored her one day when Thorold was out of hearing. 'He is mad; I know he is mad. He no longer has sane moments and I am sore afraid.'

'Afraid? Of your husband? The man you vowed to honour when you wed?'

'I am afraid of my horror, my feelings and, aye, I am afraid of him. He is no longer the man I wed. He is a stranger with devils living inside.'

Catherine was quick to disagree. 'No, he is the same man. He needs you now. When he was strong he supported you. Now he is weak and needs you to return the favour.'

'Oh, Catherine. I did not foresee this. I could not know this was to be,' I sobbed. 'People shun me. Few come to my door for healing. I sold almost nothing at the Martinmas Fair. We are destitute and I fear what will become of us.' I slumped forward and cradled my head.

In my misery I knew I had lost my robust condition. I saw the lines that tracked across my face and the grey threads that were developing in my hair, and I still a young woman. My burdens were indeed heavy and Catherine was powerless to help me. I blew my nose and wiped the tears from my face. 'I am in despair. I wish he had not returned.'

Catherine's eyes widened and she gasped. 'How can you wish such a thing?'

'It's true! I wish he had died out there on the *Falcon* with everyone else, for surely they are all dead. This is no way to live. There is no escape for either of us. We have no means of making our way in the world. I am tied to his needs. I cannot earn enough for one of us to live on, never mind two. Am I so wrong to wish he had not survived?'

Instinctively Catherine put her hands to her swollen belly as if protecting her unborn child from things it ought not hear. 'I fear it is wrong to wish it, but I cannot lay blame at your door for doing so. Perhaps Hallam could help you in your distress. You must talk to him; tell him of your feelings. There must be something we can do to ease your burdens. Perhaps the town fathers ...'

'No! Never that. I swore I would never approach the town fathers for help. I would need be in my darkest hour before I would do that.'

'Then you are not yet in your darkest hour. I shall ask Hallam to call on you.'

'Perhaps not. I will talk with him after chapel.'

'Very well, as you wish. Until then, my dear.' And Catherine left me despairing in my small croft.

~~~~~

Thorold was restive, muttering and thrashing about, waking me from a deep sleep.

'We starve for want of food and Captain Walterson, that good man, he was the first among us to die, concerned to the last for his crew. What is to become of us now? For our wit's sake, we must make our escape from this hellish place.'

'Hush, Thorold. You're dreaming again.'

'It's no dream. 'Tis a nightmare that besets us. So many lie deep in icy graves and we few who are left face Satan's worst temptation. Hunger gnaws at our bellies and Captain Walterson ...'

Thorold began sobbing, the rawness impelling me to reach out and try to comfort him.

'Don't touch me! I am unclean. I touched three men who died today, oozing with disease. God! What is to become of us?'

Thorold's outburst disturbed me. The men of the *Falcon* must have made landfall somewhere. What happened to the ship? In the darkness I ventured to speak. 'Tell me about the ship, about Captain Walterson.'

'He is gone.'

'Tell me, Thorold. What happened?'

'The men ... they are all dead and I am damned.'

'Damned? Why damned?'

Thorold cried out with raw anguish that chilled my soul. 'I am cursed beyond salvation! My sins remove me from the company of men and angels. Not even God could forgive me. I am unclean.'

I could not comprehend Thorold's meaning. His words raised many questions in my mind. What sins might he have committed in the Arctic wilderness? If he buried his shipmates when they died of starvation and disease, his feelings of being cursed and unclean might be well understood. The God I knew would not turn His back on such a man, who was guilty of nothing save surviving when others did not. I lay quietly, listening to the sobs that tore at us both, and waited for him to settle.

I wanted to talk with the Reverend about what I had heard this night. I yearned for comfort as earnestly as Thorold. But I was afraid. Thorold's nightly struggles were becoming more disturbing, more despairing, and I feared for Thorold's sanity as well as our future – and perhaps even for Reverend Tait if he involved himself in our suffering. It would be best if I kept my own counsel for the present, though it would be difficult to bear. If only Thorold would talk to me. His torment was becoming my torment. I was torn between wanting to know what had happened aboard the *Falcon* and wanting to remain ignorant. My husband was the only survivor of the voyage and was fearfully disturbed by whatever had befallen the crew. My own imaginings were growing more terrible – images of the *Falcon* crushed beneath the weight of ice, of starving men, of ravenous bears – and overtaking my slumber. There was no more sleep for me that night.

~~~~~

As the year moved into December, the first of the winter gales struck the Islands. Days and nights were freezing and, even through layers of clothing, the sting of the wind felt as if the skin was being slashed with knives. It seemed to match Thorold's black moods and my pain. Those who ventured outside struggled to stay upright against the fierce storms that shrieked from the North Sea. They hauled themselves hand over hand by whatever means they could find – fences, trees, even the scant grasses that still survived in the peat fields. Animals sheltered in the byres unable to graze, dependent on whatever miserable feed could be provided. Hens roosted as if night had fallen. A thick blanket of snow covered the fields and disguised the paths. With the fences down for the winter, I could no longer distinguish where one property ended and another began.

And then, on a bitterly cold night, we were woken by a violent gale, fierce enough to scream around the crofts and lift the thatching, mean enough to frighten the animals, brutal enough to terrify everyone cowering, vulnerable in their homes. I worried that the fishing vessels might not withstand the wild onslaught and feared what that would mean to the men who used them. I could not tell the difference between the screaming sound of the wind and the wailing of someone in distress. Many a murder might happen on a night such as this, without anyone being the wiser. I huddled beneath the covers while Thorold, no doubt thinking himself at sea aboard the *Falcon*, slumbered fitfully beside me.

The storm continued to rage through the following day, blowing and bellowing across the landscape, tearing plants from their beds, destroying whatever was not strong. Only the Lord knew what further suffering this would wreak upon Thorold and me. The storm betimes began to lose its strength, but devastation lay in its wake.

'Look, Thorold.' I pointed across the bay at the wreckage that drifted ashore from the fishing vessels. 'The herring boats. They are splintered, cast aside like waste.'

Thorold glanced at the scene of desolation and went indoors again. ''Tis nothing. A bit of a blow. That's all it was.'

'It was more than a bit of a blow. It was a huge storm and the fishermen who have lost their boats will curse it.'

'Hah!' Thorold's trumpeting guffaw was unexpected. 'Fishermen, tiddlers. They've seen nought until they've been dragged behind a whale. They've not been chafed in an Arctic storm, nor cut by the icy barber. 'Tis nothing.' Then he slumped against the table, his shoulders began to heave and great wracking sobs filled the air.

I rushed to his side. 'Thorold, what is it? What troubles you so? Please tell me.' I stroked his back, wishing to ease his torment, but he flung me away from him and stumbled to the bed, slamming the door as he went.

Our croft withstood much of the storm, with only some thatch needed in the roof and some stones in the walling, but our garden beds were destroyed and with them my chance to extend my supply of herbal physic. With the misfortunes of death and disease and now the ravages wrought upon the herring fleet, the whole community would suffer hardship. The loss of so much of the herring fleet was a ruinous blow. Folk lost wages and the means to earn them, as it was for me and Thorold. Following upon that, as a consequence, shopkeepers felt the loss of business and trade with the fishermen. Soon most households would find it impossible to buy the goods they needed and by the time winter deepened, the shopkeepers would no longer fully stock their shelves. The Islanders were plunged into poverty – Thorold and I among them. It was a bad time to be so bereft.

I was driven to struggle from door to door in the hope that I could sell remedies to those who were still suffering from the malady that attacked the community weeks earlier. I was forced to battle the weather as well as the mood of the community. Some desperate souls exchanged meagre supplies of smoked fish or eggs for my remedies. Some asked me to help them and await recompense when things improved. I felt unable to refuse. Hence, as I begged for our keep my herbal supplies gradually diminished and soon I could no longer forego calling on the town fathers for help. And all the while people continued to succumb to the deadly malady that had struck them down.

~~~~~

At chapel on Sunday, I was approached by Marian Sinclair.

'Missus Jamieson, a word if I may?'

'Certainly. How may I help?'

Marian cleared her throat and avoided my eyes as she spoke. 'It's Rhona. She shan't be coming to you for learning no more.'

'She won't? Is she alright?'

'Sure, she's well, unlike others I could name.' Marian avoided my eyes. 'I don't want to take chances, what with everyone getting sick and dying like.' She paused. 'Like Jacob says, you and Mister Jamieson still stand fit and well.'

The sting in her words clearly attested to the slight she intended. I felt as if I'd been slapped. 'Am I to take your meaning that you connect me with the sickness? With the deaths?'

'Aye. You and your amulets, your potions and oils; they didn't help, did they now? They didn't help my Harald. Nor many others I could name. I'd have better put my trust in the Lord,' she said as she made the sign of the Cross. 'So, if you please. Rhona won't be coming around. She's forbidden.'

I drew myself up and stepped in front of Marian Sinclair's gaze. 'And you feel so sure of this, yet you dare not look at me?'

We confronted one another directly. Marian folded her arms about her. 'Aye, I do. How is it that your infusions and creams and potions slaughter so many yet Thorold remains well, him who was sickening as to death? Pray, how is it? Do you dose yourselves with the same physic ... or is it the Devil's doing?'

The congregation had begun to leave the chapel but suddenly I felt the rage boil within me and it took hold of my thinking and led me to shout to all who stood nearby.

'Do you all hear this woman? Do you hear how she slanders me? Come and hear what she has to say ... if you don't already whisper it among yourselves. Do come and listen. Our beloved sister is such a fount of knowledge and wisdom, older than these barren shores. She knows so much more than you or me, even more perhaps than the Almighty Himself. No – don't you be going anywhere, Mistress Sinclair,' I said and grasped the woman's arm as she made to leave.

Parishioners gathered around the two of us and Reverend Tait soon appeared to investigate the commotion outside the chapel doors.

'Go on,' I demanded. 'Repeat what you just said to me. Tell everyone abroad what poison you scatter to the winds, what sickening untruths you whisper behind closed doors. You've said it to my face. Now repeat it so all may hear and marvel.'

Marian clamped her lips and stood unmoving while I held her fast.

'No? You've lost the power of speech perhaps?' I addressed the gathered crowd. 'I can inform you of her speech and let her deny it. Do you want to hear it?'

'Come now,' a male voice interrupted. Reverend Tait had moved through the crowd and stood close by. 'Perhaps we could retire to the chapel and talk.'

'Oh, no, Reverend, with all due respect,' I replied. 'What was said to me out here in public has no place in chapel. We will deal with it here, if you please. So, Marian Sinclair, what have you to say? Will you repeat what you said to me?'

'Let the poor woman go,' someone called from the throng.

'Aye. She's a harmless wretch who's lost her husband. You should be ashamed of yourself, heaping abuse on her like that.'

The cry was repeated, but I would have none of it. 'Is that so?' I shouted. 'And who among you have I harmed, to take her side when you have not heard what she said? Tell them, Marian. Tell them you accused me of witchcraft.'

A communal gasp was heard and people backed away, leaving us standing solitary in the centre.

'And so it is!' Marian said. 'Witchcraft it is. That's what it is. You're a witch.'

'My Lord, that you would dare say that to my face, you wicked woman!'

At that moment, Reverend Tait took hold of me and guided me towards the chapel.

'That's enough, folk. Marian, I'll be wanting a word with you today. Be sure to answer your door. As for the rest of you. There's no truth in this. Go home! Go and pray for forgiveness for even thinking such a thing.' And with that he led me to the chapel, though I was rigid with anger and huffed all the way.

104

Glennis Leith

~~~~~

Hallam made no pretence of his despair and disappointment as he led me inside.

'What possessed you to flare up so? It is unlike you, even under pressure.'

My fury had eased nary a little and I attempted to shield myself from his scrutiny. I did not meet his eyes, humiliated as I was by my outburst, yet at the same time pleased I had defended myself in public against the ill will that was surrounding me.

'It came over me of a sudden. Marian said ...'

'It matters not what she said. You know it was untrue.'

'Aye, but others believe,' I snapped. 'I have heard it from so many that hers were the last lips I needed to hear it from. You know she has forbidden Rhona to come to my croft?'

'That does not surprise me. If she truly believes you a witch she would want no child of hers to associate with you. Can you not see that?'

'Only too well. But I am not a witch. How can I fight such monstrous claims?' I felt my cheeks burn with indignation.

'By your deeds, my good woman, by your deeds.'

'And how can I do that if I am refused entry to their homes? Healing is all I know.'

'Patience. You must have patience. The Lord will be your support.'

105

'Reverend, do you believe I do the Devil's work?'

'Despite all I hear to the contrary, no, I do not believe that to be so. I see your pain; I know how hard you work. Catherine tells me of your great distress and I have seen it with my own eyes. No witch could care so about others.' He took my hands in his. 'Trust me, Inga, Missus Jamieson. The Lord's way will be found.'

I hung my head. 'I believe the gossip comes from my brother, Jacob. He claims the cattle have been blighted and the crops diseased and that I am the cause.'

'It is easy to blame others for our own troubles. Take no heed of Jacob's whisperings. They will have their own reward.'

'Do you truly believe that?'

'Aye, I do. Now, let us walk quietly to the Manse and take a cup of tea with Catherine before you go home.'

~~~~~~~

Not long after I arrived home, I heard a knock at the door. It was Jacob and I would have turned away but for his words.

'Father is unwell. Come with me now if you are to see him.'

'What's happened? How bad is he?'

But Jacob had already climbed into the trap and was holding the reins, waiting for me to join him.

The two of us spoke nary a word on the journey to the farm. Jacob was tight-lipped. I sensed that my family still saw me as a threat. The summons was a reluctant one, only on account of kinship. When we arrived, Norah was hesitant and clearly unsettled. She fussed about the house, flitting from table to door to bedchamber. Charlotte sat stitching by the fire.

'He's in there,' Norah said and pointed. 'He's poorly.'

Both Jacob and I made for the bedroom, Jacob pushing in front of me.

'I'm here, father,' he said. 'Her, too.'

'I have a name, Jacob. He is my father as well.' I spoke to Norah. 'What happened?'

Norah whispered, afraid the old man may hear. 'He breakfasted with us and went outside to do some chores. We heard him cry out and found him on the ground, clutching his chest.'

'But he's not old enough to suffer from his heart. He's only 52,' I objected.

Charlotte spoke. 'Father has been unwell for a while, Inga. I was not permitted to tell you.' She glared at Jacob.

Jacob rounded on me. 'What you've done to the family would be enough to push him into the abyss. How do you think that made him feel?'

'Don't talk about him as if he was no longer with us. I've brought some supplies with me. I'll give him something to ease his discomfort.'

Jacob leapt to his feet. 'You will not! I forbid it!'

'It is only herbs, Jacob. It is nothing that will harm him, only ease his pain.'

'How do I know that? People call you witch ...'

'It is you who calls me witch. I've heard it said in the village that you spread tales that are not true.'

'Jacob, please ...' Charlotte begged. 'Inga is our sister. Can you not show some brotherly affection at such a time?'

'She can expect nought from me.'

'Jacob! Inga! Father, he's ....' Norah's pleading voice cut through our argument.

Our father was on death's threshold, barely able to draw breath. His face was grey, the colour of lamb's wool before it is shorn, but with a sheen as if he'd been sprayed by the waters of the voe. His eyes were closed and his breathing so shallow and slow we scarce knew if he was still with us.

All at once his eyes sprang open and it seemed for all the world as if he'd seen something beyond us four gathered at his bedside. Then, just as suddenly, he closed them again and took his last breath.

Immediately Jacob crossed himself, then stood abruptly and ordered me out of the house. 'You've seen him. Now get out. Get in the trap.'

Charlotte sat beside the bed and wept, while Norah stood beside her husband. I felt my anger rise again as it had when I confronted Marian Sinclair. 'I want nothing from you. You are poisonous, you and yours. You can bury our father alone. You'll be getting no help from me.'

'And none will be given you, should you ask.'

'I'll never ask, if I was to be dying.' I left the house with brisk steps, spitting on the threshold as I passed. 'There. If you believe me a witch, may you be cursed.'

Norah gasped and rushed to slam the door against evil spirits while Jacob bellowed oaths that rang in my ears as I made my way home.

I instantly regretted the manner of my parting with Jacob. I knew, as soon as I cursed the house, that Jacob would add this tale to the gossip he was spreading about me. I had added another burden to those I already carried. Now, the only friends I had in the world were the Taits.

CHAPTER EIGHT – *Religious Observance*

It was as if the world had closed the door on me and left me stranded with nowhere to go. For weeks the Islands were hushed and shrouded with snow. It felt to me as if the whole world was shocked at my outburst and had withdrawn to safety. The frozen waters of the voe trimmed the edge of the white landscape with silver. Here and there dark weathered stones of rig walling could be seen threading their way like buttons across the fields. The only brightness in our lives was the promise of Yuletide, now only days away, though Thorold and I could expect little merriment.

At this time of year, folk gathered whatever greenery they could find and decorated their homes. Every year I tried to bring the spirit of Yuletide into our croft by hanging brightly coloured drapery from the mantel. This year it was especially important to maintain that ritual. Elsewhere, young folk keenly took up the notion of stealing a kiss under the mistletoe. Though mistletoe was nowhere to be found, the merrymakers were not to be discouraged and a range of substitutes were brought into service. Yuletide was a time of feasting and merriment when everyone put aside the cares that had long bedevilled them. It was a forward-looking celebration when wayward men wandered home with full bellies of brew and suffered for it the day after. Women donned their Sunday best gowns and made merry with their family, friends and neighbours. Children romped and happy voices drifted over the land. I tried valiantly to put aside my cares and absorb the sense of celebration, while Thorold continued his grumbling.

This year, when children hung stockings on the mantel, they were unlikely to be rewarded with bountiful sweets on Christmas morn. The fortunate few, whose families may have fared well during the year, might find nuts or toys in their stockings. But all this would be set aside to attend chapel on Christmas Day, when pews would be filled to overflowing and everyone would give thanks to the Lord for the gift of His Son, despite their reduced circumstances.

That Christmas, the Reverend Hallam Tait took pains to construct a manger at the front of the chapel. It was modelled in stone with barley and oats strewn about and the Holy Family was represented by figures he and his wife had made for that purpose. Close inspection revealed they were of moulded clay, hand-painted and clothed to resemble illustrations of Joseph, Mary and Jesus as might be seen in books.

'Catherine painted the models and made clothes to suit,' the Reverend announced with pride. 'I would wish that everyone remind themselves of the birth of our Lord and what it means to us all.'

It also served to remind us that Missus Tait was to deliver a child in the New Year. Despite her best efforts to disguise her condition, Catherine's forthcoming confinement was an occasion for happiness. There had been so much death and disease that the birth of a child would afford a special celebration. Some made polite reference to the forthcoming event, and embraced the couple's expectation with all the joy of close family. Though almost every family had been touched in some way by tribulation, everyone attended the Christmas Day chapel services and enthused over the rousing sermons. They went home glowing with much goodwill.

That same day I offered Thorold my gift: a knee rug made with great care. He immediately fell into a morose mood.

'I have no need of a knee rug,' he retorted. 'I am not an old man in his dotage.'

The thought had not occurred to me, though I knew his legs pained him. 'It is for comfort on cold evenings, Thorold, no matter your age.'

He shook his head and cast the rug aside. 'It is not for me.'

Perhaps it was my downcast face that made him look at me and whimper. 'Choose one of my pieces for yourself for Christmas,' he said, his voice muffled by his unkempt beard.

I was surprised, having had no expectation of a gift from Thorold. But I accepted his offer with great pleasure, choosing a whittled whale as my gift.

'Thank you, Thorold. I will hold this figure dear.'

The remainder of the day passed peacefully, as did what was left of the year. A week later, New Year was celebrated with even more jollity and rather less religious fervour. Everyone was keen to cast off the old year and welcome the new with hope of better things to come. Reverend Tait celebrated our entry into 1846 with a charming New Year service that uplifted my spirits and led me to hope that our circumstances would improve.

~~~~~~

January was to be a time of celebration, for this time of year was traditional for weddings. It was a time when sailors were home from their voyages, when fishermen and farmers alike were less occupied than in other seasons, when families filled their time with sewing for their unwed daughters and people welcomed cheerful news to banish winter's gloom. The date had been set for Charlotte's wedding to Laurence Gifford and it presented a ray of light in the depths of winter. Laurence's wife had suffered a deadly fever after birthing and Laurence would have struggled to raise the bairns alone if not for Charlotte's devotion. Charlotte had asked me, as her only sister, to stand beside her at the chapel and be her witness. Jacob at once launched into a series of stormy objections that reduced her to tears and sent her scurrying across the fields to my door.

'Inga, what shall we do?' Charlotte sobbed. 'I want only you for my witness, yet Jacob is so angry and I don't understand.'

I drew her to a chair and tried to explain. 'Jacob and I fell out. He accused me of dealing with the devil and ...'

'Our brother?'

'Aye. And more besides. You've heard the whispers around these parts, of witchcraft and such things?'

She sniffed and straightened her shoulders. 'I don't credit such nonsense.'

'Jacob spread it about. He and father questioned why Thorold and I remained hale when others were taken by disease. They blamed me for the cattle blight.'

'Both of them?'

I nodded. 'It seemed Father was convinced by Jacob's talk.'

'Jacob's attitude puzzled me, the day Father passed away, and you were so angry.'

'And rightly so.'

She hung her head again. 'What are we to do now, Inga? How can we make him see that you are not to blame?'

'I doubt that we can, my dear girl. He has it fixed in his head and ...'

A thunderous pounding on the door startled us both.

'Charlotte! Come outside!'

'It's Jacob,' she whispered.

'You will come home right now. Charlotte! I know you're there.'

'You must go. You cannot be drawn into this. It is between me and Jacob.'

'But I will have you as my witness. I will.' She rose and moved to the door. 'Here I am, Jacob. What is it you want?'

'You will not set foot in this house ever again. Do you hear me?'

I stood behind Charlotte at the door and faced my brother.

'I believe Charlotte is to be wed and you will no longer be her authority.'

Jacob's face was the colour of beet. He grabbed Charlotte by the wrist and pulled her outside.

'Jacob! You're hurting me.'

'You would sink to this, then?' I said.

'This house is bewitched,' he said, ignoring me. 'You will stay away.' He tried to drag Charlotte to the trap that stood waiting.

'Inga is my sister. I will have her as my witness, Jacob.'

'You will not!'

At that, Charlotte stamped her foot and wrenched her arm away from him. Now it was she who was angry. 'How dare you! If Father were here ...'

'He would command you as I do.'

'Your argument is with me, Jacob, not with Charlotte. Leave her be.'

He swung around to face me. 'For you to besmirch her good name? I will not allow it.' He reached again for Charlotte's arm but she backed away from him.

'Nothing I do could tarnish Charlotte's reputation. But your actions do you no credit, nor any who live under your roof. Think on that.'

He raised his hand as if to strike me, but at Charlotte's horrified gasp, he thought better of it.

'If this witch supports you at your marriage, expect no dowry from me.'

'I will be well provided for,' Charlotte replied. 'And Inga will stand with me at my wedding.'

'Be it on your own head, then,' he growled and swung up into the trap, urging the pony to a fast trot as he left.

'I am sorry, Charlotte. It will be unpleasant for you now.'

'No matter, Inga. I am soon to wed. Jacob will not stop me from having you as my witness, I swear it.'

'I have long wished it.'

We hugged one another and went indoors to regain our composure before Charlotte would be obliged to return to the Magnusson farm. Now, at least, I had the wedding to anticipate, despite Jacob's attempt to interfere. I was pleased that Charlotte had defied our brother and insisted on my presence. It gave promise for her future that she stood by her beliefs and would not be swayed.

~~~~~

The day of the nuptials dawned dark and dreary, but my spirits were high, rejoicing for the young couple. I would have wished Thorold to accompany me but, though circumstances denied me that, I was grateful that at least I would be there for the ceremony. I wanted the occasion to be joyful and blessed. The hour approached and I donned my best gown and made my way to chapel. Relations between me and Jacob remained distant and, on my arrival, he and Norah moved away and turned their backs to me as if ignorant of my presence. I set my jaw and determined to be civil.

'Good day, Jacob, Norah. A happy occasion, is it not?'

Norah turned towards me, startled, her eyes then glancing swiftly at Jacob for direction. Jacob took her arm and moved away. I could do nought but smile politely, as if nothing untoward had occurred, and move into the chapel to await the bride.

Reverend Tait stood at the altar, ready to join Laurence and Charlotte in wedlock. Laurence's brother William, an older man, stood solemnly beside the groom who fidgeted with his tie, then with his coat, then with his hair, to assure himself all was well. I greeted them both and made to sit beside Laurence's kin. 'May I?'

'Of course, my dear. Not much room on the Magnusson side with those unruly girls,' Missus Gifford replied with a chuckle. She watched Morna and Georgina poke and prod one another and chatter between themselves and their parents. 'They're a handful, no doubt,' she added with a soft 'tsk, tsk,' to emphasise her meaning. Jacob and

Norah could not have failed to hear the comment, but sat in stony silence on the other side of the aisle. I had no doubt Missus Gifford had heard the exchange between me and Jacob and was grateful that she, at least, appeared to welcome me without judgement.

Moments later Charlotte appeared and walked to the altar in a fine gown of her own making. Her bonnet was bright and jaunty and the curls that surrounded her smiling face were glossy. She made a picture of happiness and Laurence's smile when he saw her gladdened all our hearts. These two young people were truly in love and all could see it. I stood beside Charlotte and squeezed her tiny hand before the Reverend Tait began to exhort the parishioners to attend to the formalities.

'Let us bow our heads in prayer.'

It was cold standing at the front of the chapel. I was obliged to silently shift from foot to foot, as quietly as I could, to keep from freezing on the spot. Charlotte, standing beside me, shivered, whether from cold or excitement I could not tell.

The nuptials were as formal as the intent: prayers were said, all assembled were urged to honour the duties of wedlock, lessons were read, and hymns were sung, softly at first, then lustily in celebration.

At last it came to the vows. Everyone was still and hushed as the Reverend intoned: 'Laurence Thomas, do you take Charlotte as your lawful wedded wife?'

'I do,' he replied, his voice firm and warm.

'And Charlotte, do you take Laurence Thomas as your lawful wedded husband?'

'I do,' she replied, turning to smile at her groom.

I barely heard the remaining words, my heart was so full of happiness and my eyes were filled with tears of joy.

Some jolly person thought the ringing of a handbell was an appropriate way to mark the occasion and the sound echoed around the chapel while the parish register was signed and witnessed.

Some parishioners apparently thought the bell an affront to a formal occasion and their murmurings drifted around the chapel. Eventually, the Reverend Tait signalled for the ringing to stop and introduced Mister and Missus Gifford to those assembled. The newlyweds made their way outside and hearty congratulations were offered. Smiles were plentiful and I had an opportunity to hug my dear sister who was now a married woman.

'I wish you and Laurence well in your marriage, Charlotte. May you both be blessed.'

'My dear Inga. You are so precious to me. You are always welcome in my home.'

I felt my eyes fill again with tears at her invitation. At least some family stood by me in my troubles.

The air was chill and people began to move away. Hand in hand, Laurence and Charlotte left to begin their wedded life, while the rest of us went to our own homes and reflected on the happy event.

~~~~~

With the Christmas season passed and the New Year well established, it was time to begin preparations for the Uphelly Night festivities, a celebration close to the hearts of all Shetlanders. Most of us were of Scandinavian stock and loved the ancient festival that marked the end of January and heralded the last month of winter.

On the Sunday before Uphelly Night, parishioners gathered at the chapel to acknowledge the passing of the Festive season. A parade of flickering candles moved to the front where the Reverend waited to give his blessing. While every effort was made to ensure the candles were held upright, one was tilted by an unsteady hand and wax dripped down the side, raising a stir of fear amongst those present. A repeated murmur of 'A death to come,' rippled among the people who looked at one another as if they might each be marked for the grave. The portent cast sudden gloom over everyone present. We had already lost many to the malady that afflicted the Islands, but the sickness still had occasion to strike at random and take sufferers within days. Everyone in the community was achingly aware of how fragile life was and watched fearfully for any sign of the illness. But despite the portent, youths eschewed the whisperings of others and prepared their masks for the coming night.

Young men knew that, come spring, unless they found a safe hiding place, they would be press-ganged into naval service. Most chose the alternative of signing on to a whaling crew, a choice not always to be envied, as I might attest. Either way, the Uphelly Night was a last opportunity to run wild. As night fell, the Islands were roiling with rollicking, brawling men, whose carousings disturbed the peace of gentlefolk who tried in vain to ignore the bedlam at their doors.

Eventually, most people gathered outside and watched the antics as the revellers pranced about, blowing horns, beating drums and firing guns until everyone's ears rang with the cacophony. Thorold was reluctant to watch the fanfare, becoming increasingly agitated as the night wore on and the revellers made their way towards the town.

'Do come and watch, Thorold. It is as jolly a time as we are likely to enjoy for a while,' I said.

'Leave me be,' he snapped and retired to the ben end of our croft, leaving me to observe events alone.

All night there were fights and shouts as tin kettles were brought into the fray, along with much drinking and loud uproar. From time to time, householders were accosted by unruly youths, but good nature saw most unmolested. I was glad of a reason to stay up and watch the frolic.

At one point during the night, someone decided it was time for tar barrelling to liven up the proceedings. Rival groups of youths built frames that carried barrels of hot tar from the docks. The barrellers stirred the molten contents as they pulled and dragged the barrels along well-trodden paths towards the town and through the streets, yelling and brandishing sticks that steamed with tar, endangering any who chanced in their path. Their shouts filled the air and the smell of hot tar filled my nostrils. The smell was unfamiliar but not unpleasant, reminding me of burning molasses, though this, too, was something I had not encountered since childhood.

The practice of tar barrelling was risky, endangering both life and limb, but it drew a smile from me. The surfeit of energy and mayhem was a palliative to my sorry state. Every year, the town fathers appointed special constables to limit the chance of injury or damage to property, but to no avail. After the melee, some buildings were damaged, the paths were a mess and some even impassable. Many revellers suffered burns and other injuries as a result of the mayhem but tended to their own wounds. Sorry they were when dawn finally broke, but I could not but be cheered by the night's festivities. All the following day, while Thorold slept, I concentrated on routine tasks until I, too, folded onto a chair and fell asleep. It was the most refreshing rest I had experienced for some weeks. Later, Thorold and I ate a quiet meal and I took some time to read before once again retiring to bed.

Next morning I could hear the animals restively moving about in the byre, so I rose and stirred the fire, heated broth from the day before and quickly made bannocks. I made my way to the byre with its stone walls, timbered roofing and driftwood cattle stalls that glistened with condensation. My first task was to clean out the cattle stalls, shovel dung from the peat flooring and remove it to the outside midden. I checked the waste drain behind the cattle to make sure it was running freely to the outside and then to a nearby burn that ran to the sea. Hanging the kollie lamp on a peg, I tethered the first cow and began milking her, leaning my head into the animal's warm hide as I squeezed milk into the pail. After I'd finished milking, I attended to the horse and hens, collected eggs and returned to the but end of the croft. It was still dark.

Another day indoors, trying to keep warm with barely enough to eat. Thorold tossed abed, and I wondered what I might do to help his growing agitation. As if in response, I heard the sound of a pony and cart, followed soon after by a knock at the door and a man's voice.

'Inga. Are you there? I can see the lamp.'

'Hallam?' I opened the door and fetched him inside. He stood shivering as he shrugged snow from his clothing, his flushed face and glistening eyes evidence of excitement.

'Can you come? It's Catherine. She's in labour.'

Catherine wasn't due to deliver until mid-March. This was more than six weeks too early. 'What happened? Are you sure she's in labour, Hallam?'

'Yes, yes. She's bleeding and is discomfited. She asked me to fetch you.'

I felt anxiety begin to rise. 'It's too soon, Hallam.'

Hallam misunderstood. 'I grant you it's early and I'm glad to find you about, but ...'

'No, I meant it's too soon for the birth. It's not yet her time. The baby isn't ready.'

Hallam's breathlessness had begun to ease, but now he held his breath. 'You mean …?'

I quickly debated with myself whether to tell him there were risks for both Catherine and the baby with an early delivery. The chances of the baby's survival would be particularly slender.

'I won't know until I've checked her. It may be possible to ease her discomfort, but there are no guarantees, for her or the baby, not when it's this early. Now would be a good time for prayer.'

Hallam tensed and began to fidget, appearing highly anxious, as well he might be.

I hurriedly flung a wrap around my head and shoulders and put on my rivlins. I glanced at the ben end of the croft. 'I don't wish to wake Thorold … we daren't waste any time. I'll leave him be and hope he'll sleep until I return.' I reached for a kishie that held a selection of preparations. 'How was Catherine when you left her?'

'Her waters …'

'Oh, Lord. When?'

'During the night.'

'I believe you're right then. It's begun.' And I rushed outside, following close behind Hallam who led the way with his lamp.

CHAPTER NINE – *A Red Thread*

It was still dark. Weak sunlight would not filter across the countryside until around nine of the clock, after an absence of eighteen hours. There was no warmth in six-hour days and the snow turned into sludge underfoot. As Hallam and I approached the Manse we could hear Catherine's moans.

We entered the modest sleeping quarters that were as sparsely furnished as my own. The room boasted a simple cupboard, a small table with a ewer and basin, and a chair that had once belonged to Catherine's grandmother. Beside a substantial wooden bed we found Catherine crouched forward, holding her belly and moaning. Her hair hung limply around her face. Several layers of clothing, infrequently removed in winter, clung to her already clammy skin. I could detect a slight tang of urine in the air and a stronger smell of musk and of blood. I rushed forward.

'I'm here, Catherine. I'm here.'

Catherine flashed me a look of gratitude. 'Thank you for coming, Inga. I sorely need your assistance.'

I turned to Hallam and marked off items on my fingers. 'Hallam, fetch me some sheets and towels and a pail from the byre.' I set the kishie on the floor and washed my hands at the basin. We two women smiled at one another, sharing a journey only we could take. Where previously Catherine had supported me, our roles were now reversed. I had a chance to repay the Taits for their kindnesses.

'Get on the bed, Catherine. I need to see how far your confinement has progressed.' Catherine complied and rested quietly, knees drawn up, while I gently felt her belly, trying to detect the position of the baby. It was clear her confinement was well advanced. I straightened, put my hands on my hips and tried to reassure her. 'Well, my dear. We'll be welcoming a bairn into the house before long. We have a job of work to do.'

At that moment, Hallam returned as bidden and set a bundle of cloths on the chair, a pail beside it.

'Thank you, Hallam. We're going to be busy here for a while. I wonder if you could heat as much water as possible, and keep the fire stoked. Perhaps warm a blanket? We have to keep our little mother cosy. I'll call you if I need you.'

'Of course, I'll get to it right away,' he said and left the room.

'To keep him occupied,' I murmured to Catherine and we understood one another.

While Catherine stripped off some of her outer clothing, keeping a jacket around her shoulders, I spread birthing sheets on the bed, took a piece of red cloth from the kishie and tied it to the end of the bed to ward off evil spirits. Catherine got onto the bed and settled herself.

'Ahh!' She gripped the mattress, drew up her legs and rolled onto her side. She was uncommonly pale and her dark eyes seemed to grow larger in her face, so deep were the shadows around them.

I was troubled by her lack of colour, but tried to keep my voice calm. 'When did it start, Catherine?'

'Some hours ago. I cleaned the house from end to end on Tuesday, and yesterday my back ached all day. I couldn't get comfortable. I thought I must have strained it.' Her breathing eased a little and she paused for a moment. 'Then yesterday I couldn't eat any dinner and felt my belly drawing tight. I thought I'd rest a while and perhaps the feeling would go away. But I got up during the night – I was mightily thirsty – and my waters broke. The pain has been constant since then, and gets worse as time passes.' She suddenly doubled up. 'Ahh! Dear Lord. It hurts.'

'It's best not to strain, Catherine. Try to relax. We don't want the bairn arriving all in a rush. You need to conserve your energy.' I held Catherine's hand and stroked it while she lay moaning.

Her composure momentarily recovered, she glanced at me. 'Do you and Thorold plan to have bairns?'

'I always wanted a family,' I admitted, remembering my departed older sister. 'A few girls and a boy or two,' I added. 'But it's not something I expect for the moment with Thorold in his condition.' I reflected on the likelihood of bearing children. How could Thorold father a bairn? Do I even want to be a mother now?

'Hallam and I always wanted children. It's taken us so long, I thought it would never happen. We've been praying for this child for years.'

An intense contraction gripped her and she shrieked. I quietly checked her condition, concerned at the level of distress she was suffering.

'I'm going to give you a tisane of wild raspberries to ease your discomfort. We'll invoke the powers of St. Margaret and St. Elmo as well.' I saw a fleeting glance of wariness on Catherine's face and quickly added. 'The Lord can always use a little help, you know.'

The two of us worked in unison for what seemed like hours, perspiration glistening on both of us. Catherine tried valiantly to restrain her cries, but shrieked as sudden pain drove through her.

Hallam knocked timidly at the door. 'Is everything all right? Do you need hot water yet?'

'We're fine, Hallam. We'll be wanting a pot of tea before long. I'll call you.' I didn't take my eyes away from my friend and Hallam withdrew. This was a woman's task.

Catherine was unnaturally pale and her lips were darker than usual. 'I wonder if it's a girl or a boy,' she said. 'Hallam would like a boy. But I rather fancy a little girl.' Another spasm seized her and I massaged her belly, at the same time checking the baby's progress.

'We'll know before long. Try pushing now, my dear.'

Catherine summoned up enough energy to follow my instructions.

'This is so difficult. Why is it so difficult?' She was shedding tears as she grimaced. Her skin felt clammy and the dark moons below her eyes were deepening. She had lost a lot of blood.

'It's so for all mothers, my dear. I've no doubt I'll encounter the same when it's my turn.'

'I didn't expect it to be so hard, Inga.'

'What did you expect it to be like?'

'Something like lambing in the spring ... everything soft and sunny and warm. My baby was due in spring.'

'I know.' I massaged her belly again.

'I'm so weary, Inga. How much longer will it take?'

'Not long now. We're almost there. Push, Catherine.'

Her face screwed and reddened as she focused on her womb, grunting with the effort.

'Good. That's good. Take a breath and then we'll do it again.'

She lay panting.

'Another push, now.' I offered my hands for her to strain against. Again Catherine struggled, then suddenly relaxed.

'I can't. I haven't the strength.' She whimpered.

'Aye, you do. Come on. Try.'

She pushed and then lay panting.

'Well done. Now relax and take a breath.'

I checked progress. The baby was only moments away. Beads of perspiration ran into Catherine's eyes and dripped from her chin. Her hair was damp and clung in bedraggled curls to her neck and face. She was unearthly pale. It's the cold, I thought. She needs something to warm her blood … pepper and salt leaves to chew and then an infusion. But after the baby has arrived, not before.

'I have the head, Catherine. Just one more push and it's done.'

She lay exhausted, for all the world like an abandoned nestling.

'Push, Catherine. Come on, you can do it. One more time.'

She gathered what little remained of her strength and pushed. She screwed up her face, grunted and the bairn slipped, greasy and plum-coloured, into my hands, followed by the umbilical cord that was coiled tightly around the baby's neck.

The bairn was dead.

Catherine gazed weakly at me, a question in her eyes.

I swallowed. Then I whispered, 'It's a boy.'

Her breath was soft and quiet, the sound of a deflating balloon. 'Hallam will be pleased. May I hold him?'

I fought to hide my distress. 'I need to cut the cord.'

Quickly, I gathered the tiny boy into a towel, marvelling at his miniature fingers, the soft folds of his skin, and the mildly red lights in the tufts of downy brown hair on his head. I laid him on the bed, took some red thread I had brought with me, tied the umbilical cord in two places, swiftly severed it and tied it off.

'He's not crying, Inga. He's a quiet baby.'

'Catherine, he's ... the baby's quiet because ...' Her eyes sought mine. 'We've lost him, Catherine. The baby is stillborn.' I felt tears fill my eyes.

'No. That can't be ... it can't. I felt him in my womb, Inga. I felt him move. He wanted to be born.'

'Catherine ... the tiny soul ... he's gone.'

I gently rested the stillborn babe in her arms. One look confirmed my words and Catherine began to wail, her anguish rising from a well deep inside and washing over her child's lifeless face.

At the sound, Hallam rushed into the room, his bespectacled eyes large in his white face. 'What is it? What's happening?'

He saw his wife cradling their infant and beamed with the joy of fatherhood. As he moved excitedly towards them, I gently put my hand on his arm to stay him. Hallam stalled and looked at his wailing wife ... and realisation began to dawn. With fresh understanding, he flung himself on his knees beside the bed and wept – great gushing howls of anguish.

I stepped back, not wanting to intrude on their grief. But my misery surfaced and I, too, sobbed. This was my fault. I was to blame. How did this go so horribly wrong?

Suddenly, amidst the sobbing, Catherine began writhing and perspiring profusely, deathly pale.

'Catherine! Inga! Something's wrong.'

I rushed to her side. 'It's the afterbirth. I must remove it.' I massaged Catherine's belly, urging it to contract and expel the afterbirth. I pulled on the cord, gently at first, then more firmly and moments later the fleshy parcel released and slid away. I dropped it into the pail beside the bed, cleaned Catherine and tried to make her comfortable but she lay ashen and uncaring on the bed, blood flowing freely from her now-empty womb. Hallam was agitated and distracted, uncertain what he should do. Quickly I stopped up the birth canal with a clean cloth drenched with a decoction of campion to stem the bleeding, but soon the cloth darkened, soaked with Catherine's blood.

'What's wrong? Dear Lord, what's happening?' Hallam was trembling as if from a fever. Catherine lay unresponsive.

'She's haemorrhaging, Hallam. I can't stop it.'

'There must be something you can do.'

'I've tried.' I was distraught.

'Oh, God! No!' Hallam clasped his wife in his arms, willing her to live, but she sagged limply against him. Less than an hour later she, too, was dead.

In one stroke, Hallam had lost his child and his beloved wife. I sat quietly with him, just the two of us, each in our own way, trying to come to terms with what had happened. I found myself recalling the portent of the dripping candle at the chapel service, and silently scolded myself for thinking such thoughts.

'Isaiah. We were going to call him Isaiah.' Hallam nursed his head in his hands. 'My son is gone. I shall never have another. My future has been swallowed up.'

I felt my own despair at their deaths, deaths I had failed to prevent. How could I comfort Hallam? I had nothing to offer him that would ease his grief. I was to blame for these deaths, not some dripping candle. Hallam interrupted my thoughts.

'How can I tell my parishioners that God is love, after this? How?'

I fumbled for an answer that would soothe him, something that would assuage the guilt I felt as well. 'God has them both in His keeping, Hallam. Catherine and Isaiah are together, safe in God's heaven.'

'Leaving me to mourn them both. All that I valued has been taken from me.'

'All?'

Hallam's expression was bleak. 'It is winter in the Islands, winter in my heart. I am forever frozen.'

Hallam's words echoed in my mind as I slowly made my way back to the croft. I could still sense the lifeless baby I had held and still smell the heavy metallic odour of Catherine's freshly-shed blood. I wept again for their deaths, and for Hallam's anguish. He had indeed lost everything.

My confidence was badly shaken. The role I valued had been challenged and found wanting. I had lost my best friend and her baby and my self-belief was crushed. Perhaps it was true, what people were saying. Perhaps I was the cause of the cattle blight as well as the mystery illness that had stolen the lives of so many. Wherever I moved, death followed.

My life was in tatters. The man who was my husband, the man waiting for me at our croft, was nothing like the man who had gone whaling on the *Falcon*. The future we planned as newlyweds had been flensed of its flesh, leaving nothing but blanched bones. By the time I returned to the croft, Thorold would be awake, battling his fears anew. I asked myself, what more could go wrong? What other furies might be awaiting us?

CHAPTER TEN – *Cast Adrift*

Winter months were always the most difficult but in time of poverty, starvation and disease, difficulties were multiplied. I was faced with a decision: whether to approach the town fathers for assistance, something I had vowed I would never do, or approach Jacob for my inheritance. The land was gripped with icy fingers and, in desperation, I resolved to ask Jacob for my inheritance. It had not yet been distributed but surely he could not deny me, for it was not his to give but my right as my father's daughter, as decreed by Island law.

The day I chose to visit Jacob was one of hardship on the Magnusson farm. Jacob had risen to find more cattle dead or dying and his churlish mood was obvious the moment I saw him. He looked at me with anger flaring in his eyes and I stood still, wondering how to put my request to him without further raising his ire.

Jacob ignored me and moved to step indoors. I followed and was brought to a halt when he stopped at the doorway and snapped at me.

'What brings you here?'

'Jacob, if you please, I come to ask for my inheritance. Our father expected us to share in the Magnusson property, as the only remaining heirs. There was no distribution after his passing as is the custom. I ask that you grant me the southern fields that I may keep cattle or sheep and grow grain to feed myself and Thorold.'

'I'll grant you nothing. Begone.'

'But Jacob ...'

'No buts. I said you would get nothing and I say it again.'

'It is not yours to keep, Jacob. It is the law of inheritance, and it was our father's wish.'

'And he's not here to contradict me.'

'You would deny me my right? The only means left me to keep starvation from the door?'

'You make your bed. You lie in it.'

'Is that what the Good Book teaches you, Jacob? To be uncharitable to your own flesh and blood?'

'You are not my flesh and blood. You are the Devil's spawn. Go away.' And he slammed the door shut in my face.

'I will appeal to the town fathers for my rights, for compensation at least,' I warned through the closed door but received no response. I knew it was an empty threat anyway. Who in the town would take my side when nobody other than the Taits and my dear sister stood firm beside me?

~~~~~~~

The remaining weeks of winter felt exceptionally long and harsh to me. I was obliged to slaughter most of our hens for meat and broth. It was all that kept us alive, that and the milk from our one remaining cow. When I had but one hen left that clucked and watched me with beady black eyes like an impudent bairn, I sat at the table and wept. I had only sufficient remedies for myself and Thorold and nobody wanted my physic or my hand-woven goods. We were destitute, cold and always hungry. I was upset one morning to find Thorold whittling leather from his old shoes and chewing it. 'We are starving, boys, starving,' he said, apparently thinking himself aboard the *Falcon.* 'We will die one by one.' On hearing his words I felt doubly responsible. If I was forced to slaughter our last hen, then what would we do?

As if I had insufficient worries, in recent days I noticed something calculating in Thorold's eyes that troubled me more than usual. He sat whittling by the fire and watched me move about the croft, saying nothing but, reading from his glowering expression, clearly thinking dark thoughts. Something about the style of his watchfulness made me fearful. It was as though I was his enemy and he was planning an attack. At night, I was afraid to sleep beside him and often rose to sit by the hearth, with Thorold's much-maligned rug over my knees. Each morning I fled to the byre to milk the cow and occupied the remainder of my time in an effort to find something edible.

I recognised that our deprivation could be no worse than that suffered by the crew of the *Falcon*. How they had survived for more than a year without food in a harsh and alien environment was a mystery. I had heard stories about drastic rationing aboard ships that were trapped for a time and were forced to winter on the ice. There were tales of men who fought one another like savages for a scrap of mouldy bread that was as hard as shoe leather and as tasteless. What did men do when the stinking beef and the last scrap of bread was gone? Did they drink their own urine and eat the ship's rats as some stories had it? The thought made my stomach heave. I began to sink into a mood of black despair, fearing we would both die if our circumstances did not improve.

The last thing I wanted to do was appeal to the Parochial Board. Their resources were stretched to the limit with the number of poor and needy folk asking their help. I knew they would likely have no pity for the so-called witch and her mad husband. Thorold and I were alienated from the whole community, except for poor grieving Reverend Hallam Tait whose faithful support was a boon to my soul. But while I was grateful for his support I also worried for his health and his future. His constancy in the face of criticism could only harm his career in the church. Yet the Reverend regularly trudged over the snowbound countryside to our croft.

On this day, he arrived to find me slumped in the byre, weeping and stroking the last of our hens.

'What ails you, Inga?'

I continued stroking the hen. 'She is our last and I must slay her for food. We have nothing else left to eat.'

'I've brought you something from the Manse. It will delay that decision. Here.' He held out a basket of bread and meat.

'How can I thank you for your kindness?' I whispered, touched at his thoughtfulness. 'I have nothing to repay you with.'

'Smile for me. That's sufficient reward.'

We rose and went indoors where Thorold sat whittling beside the hearth.

'The Reverend has brought some food, Thorold. Do join us at the table.'

Thorold did not need bidding twice. He snatched at the food as soon as it was set on the board, and ate without ceremony, even snatching a morsel from my hand as I was about to eat. His behaviour led me to believe the stories I had heard about sailors fighting over scraps of food and I shuddered. But I allowed the incident to pass unremarked as Hallam and I quietly consumed what we could of the meal. When the victuals were gone, Thorold returned to the hearth and warmed himself while continuing to whittle with the short-bladed curved knife that was as sharp as any I used, all the while watching me and Hallam.

'What are your plans for today, Inga?' Hallam enquired. 'Perhaps you might offer me some assistance at the Manse if you have some free time.'

'I would be pleased to help in any way I am able,' I replied, glad of an excuse to be out of the house.

139

'Aye, begone the pair of ye,' Thorold snarled, a threatening expression on his face. 'I ken what ye're about and your day will come.'

Reverend Tait and I were both startled. 'Whatever do you mean?' Hallam asked.

'I see what you want,' Thorold said, his eyes glinting darkly beside the fire. 'But ye'll not get it,' he said, brandishing the curved knife he held in his hands.

I quickly donned my cap and shawl and slipped my feet into rivlins. 'I'm going to help the Reverend at the Manse for an hour or two.'

I didn't wait for Thorold's consent but fled outdoors, the Reverend following close behind. His expression made it clear that he was disturbed by Thorold's words and I made haste to reassure him as we headed towards the Manse.

'Pay no heed to Thorold, Reverend. He is often churlish of late and babbles nonsense.'

'Has there been no improvement in his condition?' Hallam asked as we walked. 'He appears to be somewhat withdrawn, if I may say so.'

'He is able enough in his body but bad dreams pursue and often wake him. I must need be watchful.'

'It is a wonder you have energy for your chores each day, with so little sleep.'

'His dreams do disturb me. They are so violent and ... sinister.'

'Oh?'

'He is preoccupied, almost secretive. Something about his manner makes me fearful.'

'Fearful of what?'

'Of violence, Hallam. He watches me as if preparing to attack. Always he has the whittling knife in his hand. I wonder what I could do if he were to use it against me.'

'Surely not. Why would he wish to harm you? He owes his recovery to you.'

'I doubt he feels that.'

Hallam took me by the arm as we strolled along. 'Come. Let us speak of other things. My sermon this week, I wrote it with you in mind.'

I was surprised. 'You did?'

He smiled as we approached the Manse. 'Come along. I have something to show you,' he said and ushered me through the front door.

In the parlour, Hallam drew a letter from the writing desk and held it out to me, urging me to read it.

'Hallam, it's an invitation to serve at a large parish in Edinburgh. This must please you.'

'It is certainly an honour to receive such an offer. But ...'

'But what?' I handed the letter back to him. 'You have doubts?'

'No, not doubts. It would be wonderful to serve such a large and busy parish. But it would mean leaving here and I am reluctant to do so.'

I could not hide my astonishment. 'But why? You must need be mindful of your career.' I saw he was discomfited and stopped.

'My career?' He waved away my remark. 'My life is here.'

I recalled the graves of Catherine and baby Isaiah in the cemetery close at hand and my glance in that direction was sufficient to alert Hallam to my thoughts.

'No. It is not the dead that keep me here, but the living, Inga.' He stepped towards me and took me by the hands. 'Please don't think it forward of me, but I have a purpose here, to support you – and Thorold of course – and those who have suffered through turbulent times.'

I averted my eyes, embarrassed at my response to his touch. 'There are surely others who could minister to our parish. You might seriously consider accepting the offer so generously made.'

He held my hands a moment longer before freeing them. 'I simply wanted you to know.'

I wanted to shift the focus onto something else. 'What was it you would like me to do while I am here, Reverend?'

He bustled ahead of me, leading me to the kitchen. 'I have some supplies here. I wondered if you would be so kind as to prepare a meal and perhaps take some home to share with Thorold. Let me show you.'

Later that day, back in my croft, with a freshly cooked bird and some vegetable broth, I pondered my conversation with Hallam Tait. It was not for the first time that I considered the feelings I harboured for him, and I instantly retreated from such thoughts. I was coming to hold the opinion that perhaps Hallam had similar feelings and I knew it was dangerous for either of us to surrender to them, particularly while strain existed between me and Thorold. I had promised to love, honour and obey my husband and always prided myself on keeping my promises. Yet I recognised that Thorold, also, was struggling with feelings that I could not fathom and he appeared unable to communicate. Life was presenting each of us with challenges, no matter in which direction we turned, and they appeared insurmountable.

I reflected on the only bright thing on my horizon, and that was Charlotte and her new husband. It was time I called on them, though I had little I might offer in the way of a gift. Nevertheless, I hoped she might understand my feelings and be my support.

'Dear sister! What a lovely surprise. Do come in,' she said as we entered her parlour and she fluffed out cushions on the chairs before we sat.

We talked or, rather, Charlotte talked. I was delighted to see her so embrace her new life with true enthusiasm. But then she leaned towards me in a conspiratorial fashion.

'I have some news, Inga.'

My first thought was that she might be expecting a child. But I held my tongue and waited for her to tell me.

'Laurence has been talking seriously about taking ship to Australia to start our new lives there. He is truly excited about it and so am I.'

'Australia? It is so far away,' I mumbled.

'Isn't it exciting? We have begun an inventory of what we need and our plans are well advanced.'

'Then you are indeed to be congratulated. What an adventure you will have,' I said, holding her hands to still their constant flutter, while my stomach was fluttering in their place.

This unexpected move meant I would lose the one person in my family on whom I might rely. Charlotte would be many miles away over vast oceans in a place I knew nothing about. Heaven only knew when next I might see her. If she left me, and if Hallam reconsidered and went abroad to Edinburgh, I would be left to face the future without support of any kind.

CHAPTER ELEVEN – *The Storm Rages*

The last of the season's storms raged over the Islands and it was difficult to leave the house for any length of time. Signs of spring were in the air and I looked forward to it and its promise of longed-for relief. I was grateful that Hallam paid us occasional visits, bringing with him small gifts of food and occasionally peat for the fire. I felt my pulse beat like a battle drum whenever he stood near me, and I knew the colour in my cheeks did not originate from the fire in the hearth. I had no difficulty noting Hallam's own nervousness and a surprising degree of shyness. Hallam's visits dampened the level of fear I may have held, but barely suppressed Thorold's animosity both towards me and towards Hallam. With every day that passed, in the few brief hours of thin sunlight when I was able to observe Thorold clearly, I knew that he was harbouring some awful plan. I could see it in his sudden and often furtive shifts in behaviour in my presence. It was apparent that Thorold harboured festering emotions and on occasion expressed them wantonly.

At night, Thorold and I sat beside the fire and I coaxed him to relax and take his ease, trying to soothe us both with a pot of herbal tea and a lullaby. But Thorold was not of a mind to take comfort from such simple things. He seemed like a coiled spring, waiting for some minor disturbance to trigger release of the energy coiled within him. For myself, I daydreamed about a fantasy future elsewhere, away from the roiling feelings that bubbled around me at home. I imagined myself as a free woman with nothing to bind me to duty or toil of a kind I now endured. I longed for a warmer clime where I could run free across fields of lush growth and nodding flowers. I longed as well for a full table of freshly baked bread, of berries and fruits and of rich and fatty meats and poultry and large, juicy vegetables, of cheeses and herbs aplenty. I longed for sunshine and laughter and occasionally indulged myself with such imaginings.

It was on such a night when Thorold and I sat beside the peat fire that I allowed a smile to spread across my face and at once knew it would be my undoing. Thorold leapt to his feet and struck me violently with one of his crutches, felling me to the floor.

'What have you to smile about?' he demanded, his face mottling purple with rage. 'I'll not have you mock me.'

I cowered unmoving, not daring to respond, hoping desperately that Thorold would retire to bed and forget his black mood. Instead, he took up the whittling knife and sat as if guarding my fallen figure, cradling the piece of timber in his hands as if it were a Yuletide goose, gently working it and letting the shavings drift over me. I tried shifting backwards towards the door, using my elbows for leverage, but Thorold struck out at me with his crutch, blocking my efforts.

'You'll make a juicy morsel when all's said and done,' he muttered, his expression black as he kept whittling the timber. 'There's enough peat for spit roasting, I dare say,' he went on. Did I dare believe my ears? I was dismayed that perhaps he thought the wood in his hands suitable for eating. Had he addressed me, or the timber? If he was truly mad, as now he seemed to be, what might he do?

Afraid to move, I cast around in my mind for a way to retreat with safety but could think of none. And all the while, Thorold hovered and mumbled threats and wielded the whittling knife as lovingly as if it were a treasured possession.

Then I heard a sound outside – footsteps! It sounded like boots crunching through snow. I followed their approach to our door and held my breath until there was a loud knock. From the floor, I looked at Thorold to see what he would do.

'Who is it?' he demanded.

'Hallam, Reverend Tait,' came the response.

'Go away!'

'I have news of importance to you both.'

'I said go away!'

'It will take but a minute.'

'Begone I said!' Thorold took up a bowl and threw it at the door. I heard the thud as it hit the timber and then there was silence. Thorold didn't move and I dare not shift a muscle. I imagined that Hallam had left, although I heard no footsteps move away from the door. But with no further sign of a visitor, Thorold returned his interest to me as I lay on the floor.

'What say you now, woman? Shall I carve you from top to bottom or the other way round?'

Now I could be certain of his intent. I implored him, 'Don't, Thorold. You're frightening me.'

'Ho, then. It's a different kettle of fish now then, is it?'

'Please, Thorold. I've done you no harm. Why are you so angry?'

'You'll not best me. When you are gone, I will remain!' he shouted and lunged at me with the knife.

I screamed. Suddenly there was a crashing sound as the door splintered and Hallam burst into the room.

'Stop!' he shouted and flung himself at Thorold. He grabbed the hand that wielded the knife and wrenched it behind Thorold's back. He took the knife away and set it on the table. Thorold heeled over like a stricken vessel and tumbled forward and, once he was down, Hallam sat astride his back. Thorold, meanwhile, spewed outrageous oaths that made me tremble all over with fear and I began to sob.

'Are you alright, Inga?' Hallam asked, restraining the captive man struggling beneath him.

'I think so,' I replied, trying to gather my wits together and scramble to my feet. I was shaken and distressed and could barely think. 'Thorold ... he flew into a rage without warning.'

'Have you any twine?'

'I ... I think there's some in the byre. I'll get it.' I fetched the kollie lamp and stumbled out of the room, my thoughts whirling. If Hallam hadn't come by our croft, what might have happened to me? The byre was dark and I could find no twine. But as I turned to leave I saw the length of plaited leather used to tether the cow for milking. It would have to do.

I stepped into the room and immediately felt Thorold's hairy arms around my neck, almost choking me. Hallam crouched on his hands and knees by the hearth, blood marking a deep wound on his head. He groaned and tried to rise, imploring me, 'Inga, my dear ... Thorold, he ...' He groaned and fell forward and lay still.

'I told you I was no sacrifice. I'll starve no more.'

I could barely breathe and struggled to free myself from Thorold's grasp, but he was strong and shoved me forward onto a chair. I dare not think what he planned to do. I was mortally afraid and felt sick. At that moment, Thorold struck me hard across the face and everything went black.

CHAPTER TWELVE – *Marooned*

When I regained my senses, I was bound to the chair with twine, unable to move. I saw Thorold sitting astride Hallam, who lay moaning on the ground, and he was about to strike him with a heavy stone from the hearth.

'Thorold! No!' I yelled, then immediately regretted calling out, for Thorold responded by striking Hallam's head with the stone. Repeatedly, he bashed him until Hallam went limp and blood oozed from his wounds. Thorold turned his now ugly face towards me and I feared for my life.

'What have you done?' My voice was barely a whisper. 'You've killed him.'

'Aye, and what if I have? I'll be the last man standing, mark my words.'

I wanted to flee but was unable to move. 'You've killed him,' was all I could say as I looked at Hallam in a pool of blood on the floor and I felt my heart rip apart.

'It's every man for himself. No man will make a meal of me.'

His words snapped me back to the present. 'What in God's name are you talking about?'

'Captain Walterson said to draw lots, but I'll not wait for my lot to come up. Get in first,' he said and thumped Hallam's body, as if to make certain he was dead. Then he laughed, a wicked sound that gurgled from his tormented soul. 'Like with the others,' he added.

I gaped. 'The others? You killed them?'

'Cap'n said it would save us. Haagh!' he bellowed and thumped his own chest.

My blood turned to ice. I was brought undone by the horror confronting me. 'My God!' Thorold's leering mouth and blood-red eyes spoke of madness. 'You ate them.' He simply grinned at me. 'How many?' I shrank from the foulness that knelt over Hallam's body.

'All of them.'

My face was filmed with perspiration and far colder than the chill in the air as I heard the grisly tale. Thorold still grinned at me, a sickening, malicious grin and then he howled with hideous laughter. That sound was like the hounds of hell baying at the door. The silence that followed was sharp and painful.

'So, when there were just two of you left ... you killed your shipmate.'

Thorold made a hideous sound that was half human, half animal. 'I cut his throat as he slept.' He leered at me. 'I'm no sacrifice.'

I stared at Thorold as I would a monster, for that was what he had become. Poor dear Hallam lay dead on the floor, yet another victim of the unbearable tale that was unfolding. And there, as he dragged himself to his full height, Thorold gloated at his own survival and the skills he had employed to ensure it.

'I think we'll have ourselves a bit of supper,' he said, calm as you like. 'Don't move or I'll do for you as well.'

He was capable of killing me. 'What are you going to do?' He didn't answer, just stoked the fire. I spied the whittling knife on the table where Hallam must have set it aside. It wouldn't do for Thorold to see it there and make use of it. I twisted one of my hands in its direction and slowly grasped it, as quietly as I could while his back was turned, and slipped it into the sleeve of my gown.

He stood and took hold of his crutches and moved towards the byre.

'Where are you going?'

'Never you mind. Like I said, don't move or I'll do for you as well.'

A few minutes later he returned with a peat knife. Then he knelt beside Hallam's body and, with the knife, hacked off one of Hallam's arms and set it on the fire. This then was to be our supper! The thought of what I had just witnessed and the smell of burning flesh was too much for me and I fell into a swoon.

~~~~~

When I regained my senses, Thorold was squatting in front of the fire, turning Hallam's arm, insensitive to the body that lay beside him. I feared for my own life. Was there no limit to what this man would do to survive? I shifted slightly and felt the whittling knife still secured in my sleeve. Carefully I took hold of it and began to saw at my bonds. While Thorold was occupied with the fire, I worked at freeing myself, all the while considering how I might make my escape. Eventually, I managed to cut through the twine that held me captive and tried to decide on my next move.

It was no wonder Thorold's mind was disordered. He had turned murderer long ago on that fateful voyage. It was a choice he had made, not an accident of circumstance. As he had chosen to murder the Reverend Hallam Tait. I alone was witness to this inhuman tale. I alone.

At that moment Thorold turned and saw me watching him. No doubt he did not like what he saw for I was full of disgust. He moved towards me and struck me around the head and face, again and again. I felt my skin break open, I smelled blood, I felt the sting of open wounds and begged him to stop, to let me go.

'No,' he cried. 'You're next. I'll be the last man standing, I promise you.'

Despite my sorry situation, I felt anger rise from the depths of my soul, anger at God as well as Thorold. How could God forsake all those men aboard the *Falcon*, forsake Hallam in his need, forsake me against such a man as this? Fired with fury I found the will to leap to my feet.

'No! You won't!' I cried and made to stab him. But he grabbed hold of my wrists and forced the knife from my grasp. And so God had forsaken me again.

'You will not best me!' he said, his face inches from mine, willing me to submit.

I struggled against him but he held me firm and I felt the knife slice into my thigh. 'Thorold, you're hurting me.'

He pointed then at Hallam's arm, well roasted on the fire. 'You see there? That is our supper. We will eat. Then I will tie you with sailor's knots while I sleep. In the morning, I will be the last man aboard ship.'

'You cannot murder people and get away with it.'

'I'll be the last man standing. I'm no sacrifice.'

All my fury erupted. 'You are a monster!' I screamed and remembered the plaited leather I had retrieved from the byre and put in my pocket. I flailed at him with it. I lashed at his head and face and he threw up his hands to cover his eyes. My attack took him by surprise, made him step aside and without his crutches he lost his balance. He fell to the floor where I whipped him over and over. 'You unspeakable monster! You are inhuman!' I screamed.

My fury knew no bounds as I retrieved the whittling knife, threw myself at Thorold and stabbed him again and again and again and again, until he lay unmoving and I lay spent and whimpering. I dragged myself to my feet and collapsed onto the chair. My hand ached; my limbs trembled as if with a fever. My head was pounding, full of a humming noise and I could barely see, let alone think. I knew I had myself turned killer.

Two dead bodies were on the floor of my croft. How could I explain what had happened? I was too distressed to think clearly. There was nobody left to comfort or support me in my trouble. I would have to deal with this on the morrow. I spread a coverlet over the bodies and collapsed onto my bed with no expectation of sleep.

CHAPTER THIRTEEN – *The Aftermath*

In the morning, the sun cast its feeble rays across the landscape. I rose and thought to brew a pot of tea, avoiding looking at the mound on the floor. My position was immediately apparent. While it might be expected that Thorold could attack Hallam, my own actions might not be as readily explained. I felt no glimmer of hope in this dreadful situation.

Before I had time to think further, I heard a knock at the door and felt weak at the thought of a visitor at this time.

'Missus Jamieson. Are you there?'

It was Lillian Isbister. Wearily I took myself to what remained of the splintered door and greeted her without a good deal of enthusiasm.

'Missus Isbister. How can I help?'

'Oh, my,' she replied. 'Your face. You look awful. What has happened here, my dear?'

How quickly she disarmed me. I stood surprised, then hung my head and began to weep. Lillian moved to my side, put her arm about me and led me indoors.

'Oh, no, Lillian. You may not come in. Please. Let us stay outdoors.'

'I won't hear of it. You need help, I can see that ... my goodness, what is this?' She pointed at the mound on the floor.

'Oh, God help me,' I cried and folded up in a heap on a chair.

'What is it? What is that?' she asked and moved to lift a corner of the coverlet.

'Oh, please, Lillian. Don't. It's too awful.'

She turned and looked at me, concern clearly visible. I felt shamed and hid my eyes from her gaze. Lillian came and sat beside me at the table.

'Now, my dear. Tell me what has happened in this house? I see blood and ...' She pointed at the heap under the coverlet.

I had no wish to deliver that story, yet it must be told. Might it not be best told to Lillian? I sobbed and she waited.

'Thorold is dead, Lillian. Both Thorold and the Reverend Tait.'

'What? Both?'

I looked at my torn and bloodied hands and nodded. 'There he is, he and Hallam Tait together. They are no longer with us.'

'Go on.'

'Last night, Reverend Tait called to give us some news, I know not what. Thorold refused him entry and bade him leave.'

'And you?'

'Thorold knocked me to the floor. I was unable to do anything without risking life or limb.'

'Go on.'

'I am so very thirsty.'

'Of course, my dear.' She rose and fetched some water then gently sponged my bloodied face. 'This will take time to mend. You are heavily bruised.'

'My heart and soul are bruised beyond caring.'

'Tell me, Inga.'

'Thorold attacked me. He came at me with his whittling knife. I was terrified and screamed and Reverend Tait burst through the door. He grabbed Thorold and took the knife away.'

'Brave man,' Lillian said.

'Indeed. But on my return from the byre where I had been searching for twine, Thorold again attacked me. And I saw him strike Hallam on the head.' I sobbed again, recalling that dear face in its final moments. 'He struck him dead, Lillian, again and again. Oh, Lillian, it was awful. Thorold, he laughed about it. He said he was protecting himself.'

Lillian made the sign of the Cross. 'The Devil has indeed visited this place.'

'There, in the fire, Lillian, is what he did next.'

Lillian turned and looked at the fire smouldering in the hearth. A frown creased her face but moments later she lost all colour.

'My Lord. Is that ...?'

'Yes. It's an arm. The Reverend Tait's arm. Thorold cut it off and roasted it for his supper.'

Lillian suddenly grabbed the water and drank great gulps of it.

'Forgive me. I feel unwell.'

We sat and looked at one another and tears began coursing down our faces. For what seemed ages, the two of us sat silent, no doubt thinking of the events that had so swiftly changed our lives.

'It all began with the voyage.'

'The *Falcon*?'

'Aye. You wanted to know about Robbie. I can tell you now.' I looked at her face, her own anxiety showing itself now. 'He fell from the main mast, Lillian. That is what took his life.'

'Did Thorold tell you that?'

'He often rambled in his sleep and said that on one such occasion. He thought himself aboard the ship.'

'So, at last I have something to tell the family. Thank you, Inga.' Lillian looked about her, and at the heap on the floor. 'My dear, there is no need to speak further of these dreadful things. That you are here and Thorold is not is a blessing and not to be wondered at.'

'I am so tired, Lillian. So very tired.'

'Here, Inga. Do come and rest. I will do what is needed.'

I willingly followed her urging and took to my bed. I heard her leave the croft and then I fell into a blessed sleep.

CHAPTER FOURTEEN – *Homeward Bound*

The events of the previous night were reported to the Provincial Council and were considered at length as to the outcome. I was questioned about the details of what happened, and gave as good an account as my memory would allow. My torn and bruised face supported my story and Thorold's lack of social contact spoke of his deepening madness. It was a blessing to learn that the Reverend Hallam Tait had already spoken to members of the Council on several occasions and acquainted them with his concerns about the circumstances that surrounded me and Thorold, and had also asked their advice about Thorold's developing insanity. Everyone knew how unstable Thorold had been and he'd scarce been seen for anyone to make any reasoned judgement of his capabilities. Thus it was accepted that I was not at fault in the deaths of either of the two men. Nevertheless, one crusty old gentleman berated me for not asking for help. 'Had you done so, madam, things might not have come to such a pretty turn. I'll leave you to think on that.' He had no need to fear I would forget.

Thorold's death released me from the burdens that had beset me for long months, but sorrow accompanied me every hour of the days that followed. I mourned the loss of my dear friend, Catherine, and the husband that was lost to me the moment he set sail aboard the *Falcon*. I also mourned the hope that had only recently begun to blossom in my heart, the loss of that dear friend, Hallam Tait, in such brutal circumstances. The images from that night entered my sleep, night after night. I would never forget.

It was poor weather to hold a funeral but it was the last of many, dear Hallam Tait having been already laid to rest beside his wife and child. The ground was rock solid and the gravediggers were obliged to light a fire to warm the earth beneath, sufficient to turn the soil.

The day of Thorold's funeral was no better nor worse than I expected: it was cold and bleak and threatened rain before evening. Few people chanced themselves against the elements. The service was held entirely out of doors, no prayers were said in the chapel. I stood at the graveside beside the lay preacher, with only dear Charlotte and Laurence, the diggers and one or two parishioners hovering nearby, likely curious to see the lone survivor of the *Falcon* gone to his rest, as other suffering souls had gone before. Jacob and Norah did not come, though news of Thorold's passing quickly became widely known. After the final prayer was said and I had dropped a clod of earth onto the coffin, I knelt and cast a solitary spray of dried herbs down into the grave. There were no flowers, not at this time of year, though Spring was not far away. I stood and turned away, leaving the graveyard with Charlotte and her husband, while the gravediggers completed the sad task of laying a blanket of earth over my departed husband.

Charlotte and Laurence accompanied me to the croft and supped with me. It allowed me the opportunity to talk of what happened and have someone hear me without prejudice. We also talked a little of the future though none of us could foresee what might yet occur.

Now that Thorold was at rest and I publicly mourned his loss, while privately mourning the passing of dear Hallam Tait, the community made no further attacks on me. Yet, I remained at a distance from most, other than Charlotte and Laurence and perhaps Lillian Isbister. Marian Sinclair made no move to address me, but neither did Rhona, nor any of the other widows from the crew of the *Falcon*. Those who had approached me for remedies in the midst of their troubles now avoided me as much as they had before. It was clear many considered me unclean, unworthy of their friendship.

~~~~~

A few weeks after Thorold's funeral, I approached Lillian Isbister.

'I would like to sincerely thank you for your help in my recent troubles, Lillian.'

'Not at all, Inga. I did what any might do.'

'Nevertheless, would you accept this parcel of woollen goods as my parting gift before I leave. I'll have little need of them where I am going.'

'Why, thank you. It will be well appreciated. And where might you be off to, then?'

I smiled. 'I've put myself forward to take ship for Australia. It is reported to be warmer there, with opportunities aplenty. I take my leave within days.'

It was her turn to smile. 'With your ability with remedies, you will be welcome, I'm sure.' She paused. 'Though you will be sorely missed here.'

'By some, perhaps.'

'By me, indeed, Missus Jamieson.'

'Thank you, Lillian.'

'God speed, Inga.' She stepped forward and gave me a quick hug, then smiled and clasped the bundle of woollens to her as I turned towards home.

Charlotte and Laurence had told me they were taking the bairns and sailing for Australia and they invited me to join them. I accepted without a second thought.

Now as I walked home to the croft, my step was light, my mood lifting as I went. The Shetlands would always be home to me, but they would always cause me pain in the remembrance. I had new horizons to seek, new paths to explore and I was free to do so. Perhaps I would yet run through fields of flowers and set a goodly table from a fine harvest. Perhaps I would yet find sunshine and laughter. Spring was almost upon us and, while the croft was my home and the fields around it were familiar to me, there was nothing to keep me in the Islands. My future lay elsewhere and I was ready to greet it.

ABOUT THE AUTHOR

Glennis has pursued an interest in writing from an early age. She is a prize-winning author who has had articles, short stories and a family history published as well as a novel for middle readers.

She reads widely, but prefers to read murder mysteries, which means most of her stories have a dark side. This book is no exception.

You may contact her through her website at
www.glennisleith.com